VAN HA

The New Wife

The Human, AI, and Alien

First edition

ISBN: 979-8-9987068-0-6

This book was professionally typeset on Reedsy.
Find out more at reedsy.com

"To my dear father, who taught me the profound truth of forgiveness—a lesson that continues to shape my heart and guide my path."

Contents

Acknowledgments

I'm thrilled to share some wonderful news—my book is now published! This achievement wouldn't have been possible without the incredible support of the team at Reedsy. Their free online courses and resources guided me every step of the way, helping me turn a simple idea into a tangible reality ready for the world. I'm especially grateful for their dedication to empowering first-time authors like me. Their expertise made the journey from draft to publication not only possible but also deeply rewarding.

This book is deeply personal, centered around the theme of losing a loved one. Since you passed away, my thoughts have been filled with dreams and memories of the time we shared. I often find myself reminiscing about moments from my childhood, like when you'd bring home hot, freshly baked baguettes and spread them with rich American butter, feeding our family with so much love.

I still recall that night in Da Nang during the war, when the artillery shells rained down on the city, and the suffocating heat inside our sandbag bunker became unbearable. Desperate for relief, I slipped outside and fell asleep beneath the open sky. You searched relentlessly, never giving up, until you found me. The joy on your face as you lifted me into your arms, knowing you had kept me safe, is something I'll never forget. You were our protector, the one who shielded our family from the chaos around us.

I also remember the time when I ran away from home, and you spent months searching for me—scouring towns, even checking youth detention centers. I was such a rebellious kid, but your capacity for forgiveness was boundless.

There's also that haunting memory of us on a rickety boat, carrying more than 50 refugees, drifting on the unforgiving ocean for days. Your face, smeared with black grease, looked up at us, your eyes filled with hope as you worked tirelessly to fix the boat's mechanical failure. In that moment, your determination became a beacon of hope for all of us, a symbol of resilience in the face of overwhelming odds.

Our reflections on the existential meaning of life linger persistently, as you and I grapple with the question of how to communicate with loved ones who have left this world behind. If the Lord is indeed all-powerful, omnipotent, and compassionate, surely, He could grant us the means to connect—to speak or write to one another, even as we exist in separate realms and forms. Is such a request too much to ask? What we long for is not a superpower ability or a miraculous intervention, but simply the opportunity to correspond with those we cherish most. In this way, you taught me to question the absolute dogma, to seek understanding beyond blind acceptance, and to find meaning, even in life's greatest mysteries.

And so, I hope this book reaches you through the collective consciousness of the millions who read it. While we may not be able to communicate as two individuals-like two entangled electrons-I believe we can connect through the shared thoughts of countless minds, creating a universal wavelength that transcends spacetime and dimensions. In this way, my words may find their way to you.

This book is my heartfelt letter to you, a message of love, gratitude for your sacrifices, and appreciation for your boundless forgiveness-words I never fully expressed while you were with us.

The Lost Cause

Enclosed by the close quarters of his studio, a space densely populated with wires and circuit boards, Thang Trinh's brow creased in profound focus as his fingers executed a rapid-fire sequence across his laptop's keys.

"Easy, brah, we're almost through their firewall," Ivan murmured, hunched over his own rig from somewhere in Eastern Europe. The flickering glow of his monitor cast shadows across the small studio lair that reeked of stale cigarette smoke.

Thang didn't look up from the lines of malicious code streaking across his screen. "I must try this out. This could be our greatest breakthrough and the biggest payout yet."

Within the close confines of his studio-home in Danang, his eyes briefly rose to their wedding photo. The once-radiant image of his wife offered a stark contrast to the fatigue etched on her face as she returned from the textile factory.

The distinct squeak of the front door announced Thao Le's arrival after the day had surrendered to twilight. Thang's gaze, previously absorbed by the complex lines of code on his laptop, rose instantly, his eyes seeking out her radiant smile—a luminous beacon that shone brightly despite the subtle signs of her growing frailty. Though the fullness of her features had diminished, leaving a delicate gauntness, her dimple-deep smile, a constant and unwavering source of confidence, enveloped him with warmth as she purposefully moved towards the small kitchen, her arms burdened with bags of groceries, determined to prepare their evening meal.

Thao slipped into her well-worn sandals, and with a gentle flick of her wrist, brushed a few stray strands of her silky black hair away from her face. Despite the now-pronounced sharpness of her cheekbones, her dimples, deeply etched with an expression of unconditional adoration, punctuated her wide grin as she began to unpack the fresh chicken, rice noodles, and a colorful assortment of vegetables.

"How was your day at the factory, Em Yêu?" Thang felt a pang of fresh guilt. His chest tightened seeing how little weight she carried on her body.

"The usual dreadful grind," she laughed softly, that ever-present warmth filling their modest kitchen. "But the promise from my husband and our purpose make any struggle bearable."

"Our uncles and generations before us struggled and defeated the colonial imperialists. Now it is our turn to struggle against corporate capitalism," said Thang as he fiercely typed codes online, sharing information with other hackers in Eastern Europe.

After an hour passed, Thang came to the dinner table as Thao brought out two bowls of chicken noodle soup. He tasted the broth and nodded approvingly, "Just like how it was made in the North of Hanoi." Thao came and sat at the table, saying, "I skipped the rock sugar so it would taste like your hometown pho. As for me, being from the south, I prefer sweeter over savory in the broth."

They ate and talked at the dinner table, discussing Thao's health issue and Thang's inspiration for making money by cyber hacking to help with the family's finances.

Thang consumed the whole bowl of noodles without even a little broth left, moving his seat next to Thao. "We're getting closer to bypassing WestCorp's firewall. Ivan thinks if we inject this new suite of exploits into their mainframe, we could syphon a fortune in cryptocurrency."

Thao's gaze, those probing, soulful eyes, settled upon him, unwavering. A deep-dimpled smile, a testament to her stead-fast devotion to his ideals, illuminated her face.

"Em Yêu..." Thang rose and wrapped his arms around her tiny waist from behind. "You know I'll do anything—go scorched earth against the entire corrupt system, close the gap between the rich and poor, and keep you healthy and by my side."

Turning within his embrace, Thao cupped his stubbled cheeks, her touch, though her frame was visibly withering, still charged with the vibrant energy of life. Her expression remained steadfast, unwavering, despite the many promises of success that lingered tantalizingly close, yet perpetually out of reach.

"I know, Anh à. And I believe you have the ability to provide for our family and our community," she kissed him on the forehead.

Tears stung Thang's eyes as he crushed her delicate form against his chest, breathing in her jasmine essence. A lump constricted his throat as he whispered the solemn vow:

"Always and forever, em yêu. Our love will be my revolution's burning heart until the end."

Neither dared to acknowledge the chilling premonition of the end that might arrive with terrible swiftness.

A few days later, Thang found himself staring down at the grainy scan image, the smudged blacks and grays blurring into an incomprehensible tableau. His doctor's pronouncement echoed in his mind, a somber death knell.

"I'm so sorry, Mr. Trịnh Thắng. The chronic lymphocytic leukemia cancer…it's reached stage four and has spread too aggressively for our treatment facility to manage." Dr. Nguyen spoke the words delicately, but they still felt like a hammer blow to Thang's gut.

"This cancer has been in her for years. Our hospital received were many patients having this cancer came from the areas of Binh Dinh and Da Nang, where Agent Orange had been absorbed in the soil." Dr. Nguyen continued to share his experience.

"Yes, I heard from my mother-in-law that her father also had the same disease, and he was a soldier stationed in Phu Cat Airbase during the war." Thang

He looked up with wild, pained eyes at the elderly physician. "There… there must be other options? Experimental treatments, clinical trials, anything?" His voice strained to a desperate rasp.

Dr. Nguyen clasped his hands solemnly. "Our best remaining hope is to get her into a cancer treating hospital in America as soon as possible. Their cancer research campuses have novel immunotherapies that may be Thao's only chance."

The premier cancer treatment facility in the world—its cutting-edge reputation inextricably linked to an exorbitant price tag. Thang closed his eyes, a wave of nausea roiling within his belly, as his mind desperately navigated the treacherous landscape of their dwindling finances.

"H-How much…?" he managed to choke out. He already suspected the answer.

"For the aggressive regimen, Thao would require?" The doctor's face tightened with mournful sympathy. "I'd estimate somewhere in the range of three to four hundred thousand American dollars, Mr. Trịnh Thắng. And that's just to start."

The room began to spin with disorienting violence. Three... four hundred thousand? He and Thao had relentlessly scraped and clawed; their meager savings barely sufficient for her treatments at the local clinic. Those paltry figures, however, were a universe away from the astronomical costs demanded by the renowned cancer center.

Thang felt a profound sense of fragility, as though his very being had turned to glass, shattering into a thousand jagged pieces upon the cold floor. This reality seemed impossible, an unbearable cruelty—not to his beautiful, vivacious Thao, the radiant light that illuminated his existence.

Amidst the swirling chaos of his spiraling panic, a familiar, defiant voice ignited within him—the same unwavering voice that had fueled a decade of cyber-activism, of redistributing wealth from the affluent to the impoverished, of battling oppression and the relentless avarice of corporate giants.

This time, however, the battle was waged for something infinitely more precious, transcending any mere ideological crusade.

Dr. Nguyen looked at him sadly. "I hope you understand the stakes here, Mr. Trịnh Thắng. If we can't get Thao to the U.S. and start immunotherapy immediately, I...I don't know if she'll make it to the next Tet."

Thang simply nodded, his throat constricted, rendering him speechless. He understood precisely what hung in the balance—his entire world, his very essence, teetering precariously on the edge of being irrevocably torn away. As he departed the doctor's office, each step felt leaden, burdened by the suffocating weight of impending despair.

Yet, within him, that defiant inner voice ignited, flaring into a roaring wildfire of determination. Months later, beads of sweat glistened on Thang's brow, the bluish glow of the laptop screen reflecting in his feverishly intense eyes. His fingers danced across the keys, a blur of furious typing.

"You're sure about this score, brah?" Hacker Ivan scratched his scraggly mane and, in a heavy accent of Eastern European origin, "Messing with WestCorp's servers is like pissing on a plasma field. Dangerous as hell."

Thang offered no response, his entire focus consumed by the intricate task of infiltrating WestCorp's servers. A mere handful of keystrokes, a final flourish of cyber black magic, and they would breach the digital vault of the corporate behemoth.

"Just a few more exploits, and we're in," Ivan muttered, jaw clenched as he rapidly deployed a new virus into WestCorp's network. "Intel says their cryptocurrency coffers are sitting fatter than any moneylenders."

A tiny muscle twitched in Thang's hollow cheek. He slowly dragged on the harsh Vietnamese cigarette clenched between his lips, imagining the choking plumes were WestCorp executives gasping for mercy.

"And if we pull it off?" His voice was barely more than a gravelly rasp. "You telling me that's enough to cover Thao's... her treatment costs? In America?"

The unspoken words, laden with a suffocating weight, lingered in the damp, close air. The MD Anderson Cancer Center's pioneering clinical trials, Thao's last bastion against the virulent spread consuming her body, offered a sliver of hope. Yet, its astronomical billing loomed, a nightmarish counterpoint.

Ivan's brow furrowed, etched with concentration, as he rapidly calculated the potential cryptocurrency payout from the planned heist. After a tense, drawn-out moment, he shook his head grimly.

"Maybe...maybe enough to cover initial admittance and a couple of rounds of therapy. But it's gonna take multiple monster raids to fully bankroll the long-term costs, brah."

A low, animalistic growl rumbled deep within Thang's chest. His hand clenched convulsively around the cigarette, the tremors threatening to snap it cleanly in two. He could ill afford to fall short, even by a single dollar, of the obscene price tag affixed to Thao's treatment.

Each passing day, her image grew weaker, thinner, her inner radiance slowly being extinguished, like a flickering candle flame projected from their wedding photo. If he were to fail here, he might as well begin composing her final rites himself.

"Then we push ahead and hit them with everything we've got," Thang growled, stabbing the final exploit keystrokes with cold, ruthless precision. "WestCorp's fortune is just a down payment. Those corrupt butchers have it coming after what they've extracted from millions like us."

On his screen, strings of malicious code, like an insatiable swarm of locusts, rapidly infiltrated WestCorp's servers, devouring firewalls and cyber defenses. But, with equal swiftness, a crimson WARNING began flashing, signaling the activation of WestCorp's formidable counter-hacking protocols.

"Aw shit...!" Ivan scrambled to erect digital countermeasures, but it was too late. Within moments, their entire rig was bombarded by WestCorp's cyber retaliation strikes.

The sickly computer screens flickered with parasitic lines of scrambled code, followed by an ear-piercing shriek of maximum feedback that assaulted their headsets. Finally, both systems crashed under the weight of WestCorp's devastating counterattack, their monitors freezing on fatal error messages as networks failed catastrophically, leaving only the deathly silence of digital annihilation.

Coughing violently, Thang slammed his fists onto the desk, the force sufficient to crack the cheap laminated surface. He threw his head back, unleashing an unholy scream of rage and despair that reverberated through the ramshackle studio-home. His grand cyber-heist against WestCorp had failed spectacularly.

Worse, their hacker crew's virtual fingerprints were now glaringly visible, certain to trigger an Orwellian security crackdown. After the choking black cloud slowly cleared, Thang staggered to the corner and crumbled against the damp concrete wall. Drops of sweat and tears mingled in streaks down his cheeks as he sobbed hoarsely into his trembling hands. He had failed Thao once again, and this time, the consequences were measured in her precious, fading life.

The studio was shrouded in suffocating silence and acrid smoke. Thang sat motionless at his workbench, staring blankly at the charred remnants of his hacking rig. The failed WestCorp heist played on a nightmarish loop in his mind's eye. With a sudden burst of manic energy, he swept the scorched computer components off the desk with a primal roar. Blackened circuitry and melted plastic scattered across the damp concrete floor.

As the echoes of his anguish faded, Thang's bloodshot eyes landed on a curious anomaly—the corner of a plain white envelope peeking out from under his keyboard. With trembling fingers, he plucked it free, feeling an unexpected weight within. His breath caught as he opened the envelope, sending a cascade of crumpled đồng bills spilling across the desk.

The faded currency carried the distinct sour tang of age and grime. Thang's vision swam as he tried to mentally tally the sum—easily hundreds of millions of Vietnamese đồng, more money than he'd ever held at once in his life. But how...where did this fortune materialize from?

A tiny scrap of notepaper fluttered free from the emptied envelope. Thao's unmistakable elegant script danced across it:

"Anh yêu, I've saved this for you, my brilliant love. To fuel your last hurdle and to achieve your revolutionary fire. Never let it be extinguished. Your eternal spark, Thao."

Thang felt the air evacuate from his lungs as if he'd been plunged into a vacuum. Hundreds of millions of hoarded đồng – Thao had been squirreling this away for ages.

All those times, she'd brushed off her progressively worsening symptoms, claiming they didn't have enough to visit the clinic. Each instance, she'd come home from the factory, smiling through her obvious exhaustion and pain, gently encouraging him to keep crusading with the hacktivist endeavor.

In soul-shattering clarity, Thang realized the obvious truth. Thao had been secretly funneling every spare penny into his cyber-activism for years – at the expense of her own critical medical care. Tears blurred the note's script into a psychedelic smear.

With a piercing wail of grief and regret, Thang clutched the money to his chest, great wracking sobs contorting his wiry frame. How could he have been so blind? His stubborn pursuits had literally drained the life out of Thao – all while she silently martyred herself to fund his quixotic ideals.

In a burst of desperate energy, Thang jammed the đồng back into the envelope and sprinted toward the front door. He had to get to the hospital, to fall upon his knees at Thao's bedside and beg for her forgiveness. To plead with her to let him liquidate this fortune, pitiful as it was, to ease even the tiniest fraction of her suffering.

His moped roared through the narrow alleyways at a suicidal pace. Thang wove around the bewildered pedestrians and fruit carts, the envelope of money clutched in a death grip, his heart jackhammering a staccato beat against it.

Thao... His sweet, selfless wife. She was the only revolution that had ever truly mattered.

And he had to pray to any deity that would lend an ear, that he wasn't too late to finally champion her cause. The harsh fluorescent lights cast an ashen pall over Thao's withered form. Tangled in the rough hospital sheets, she appeared so fragile, a delicate ceramic doll on the precipice of shattering into countless pieces.

Thang struggled to swallow the hot lump lodged in his throat as he pulled a rigid plastic chair to her bedside. Her breathing was shallow, each rise and fall of her chest requiring a monumental effort. Yet, when her eyes flickered open, locking onto his face, an unbearably beautiful smile, a testament to her enduring spirit, bloomed across her cracked lips.

"Anh yêu..." Thao's voice was feeble but still brimmed with pure, radiant warmth. With trembling effort, she lifted her skeletal hand from the sheets, gently brushing his cheek.

Thang felt his stoic cracking at her tender touch. He covered her hand with his, hating how his calloused flesh engulfed her birdlike bones. "I...I'm so sorry, em yêu. I've failed you in every way that matters."

Her brow creased momentarily in a flicker of confusion before that warm, dimpled smile returned. Always seeing the brightest of his intentions, even when he saw nothing but utter defeat.

"That's not true, anh à. You've been my revolution, my heart's fire." She drew a labored breath, each word requiring enormous effort. "Whenever your noble quest met resistance, you swept me up and carried me through the storm beside you."

Thang squeezed his eyes shut, feeling hot tears spill down his hollow cheeks, tracing paths of grief. He recalled the nascent days of their cyber-crusading crew, the daring takedowns of corrupt corporations, the redistribution of their ill-gotten gains to the impoverished. Thao's unwavering support, her tireless dedication to his ideals, had been his driving force, his inextinguishable spark of hope.

Yet, in the end, he had failed to even provide for his own small family. The crushing weight of that failure collapsed inward, like a dying star, creating a desolate void where his very soul had once resided.

"Thao...I am so sorry. You sacrificed everything for me," he choked out, voice strangled.

"Your very life as you worked double shifts at that factory hell. So that I could chase my devoted vision."

At that, Thao's laugh emerged – frail yet somehow brimming with vibrant spirit. Even now, staring into death's void, she radiated selfless joy.

"Worked hard to support the man I love more than anything? There was no sacrifice in that, anh yêu." She beckoned him closer, pulling his hand and holding onto his ring finger. "When I go to the other side, we are still together through this ring, my darling."

Thang clung to her wasted hand, trying in vain to instill his own fleeting life force into her weakening body through sheer force of will. Her dimples creased with a fresh wave of affection.

"Whatever happens next, anh… I'll forever be with you. My soul imprinted into yours like the words scribed into a cosmic altar." She pulled his face down and crushed her chapped lips into his with surprising passion.

"My love…. Our union will be eternal."

As she settled back, her eyelids fluttered, suddenly heavy. With a supreme force of will, she reopened them, fixing him with an intensity that squeezed his shattered heart.

She stroked his unkempt hair with maternal affection. "Just promise me one thing. Never forsake your family for any ideology. And always remember, no matter what happens…I'll eternally be in any of your struggles, Anh yêu."

Thang could only nod soundlessly through his streaming tears, cradling her withered frame against his heaving chest.

Thao's lids drifted once more. Her lips curved into a sublime, peaceful smile.

"Then our union endures, anh à…" she whispered with her ardent breath. "…and I shall be with you forever."

The envelope slipped from Thang's trembling grasp, the money fluttering to the ground like the falling leaves in autumn.

Months drifted by, and Thang spent his days adrift in endless reveries, chain-smoking cigarettes as if attempting to fill the gaping chasm within him. He remained clad in his old, tattered T-shirt, emblazoned with the face of Che Guevara, the revolutionary gaze now faded and cracked from relentless wear. His eyes lingered on the wedding photo, tracing the delicate contours of his wife's face, as if by sheer force of will, he could conjure her back from the void.

The cramped studio was a mausoleum for months of sorrow. Thang sat motionless on the threadbare floor; a smoldering cigarette dangling forgotten between his nicotine-stained fingers. His hollow eyes stared unblinking at the wedding photo on the mantle, the only spark of color in the dingy grey room.

In the portrait, Thao beamed with incandescent joy, her delicate features framed by a cascade of onyx hair adorned with vibrant orchids. The traditional Vietnamese silk ao dai hugged her lithe frame, its crimson and gold hues a perfect complement to Thang's embroidered black tuxedo.

But it was their expressions that seared into Thang's broken soul—the pure, unrestrained bliss radiating from their smiles, their eyes locked in an impenetrable gaze of eternal devotion— a cruel, vivid snapshot of a future that would forever remain unrealized.

Thang took a shuddering drag on the cigarette, the acrid smoke burning his lungs and stinging his red-rimmed eyes. Months had passed since Thao drew her final breath in that cold, sterile hospital room, yet the agony of her absence still flayed him raw with each waking moment.

The wedding band on his finger had become an anchor, a constant reminder of his catastrophic failings as a husband and provider. How could he have been so utterly consumed by his hacktivist crusades while Thao slowly withered away, sacrificing her own precious life force for his futile pursuits? In the suffocating silence of the flat, Thang's tortured imagination began to flicker and twist, warping his perception of reality.

The wedding photo seemed to shimmer and distort before his bloodshot eyes. Thao's radiant smile began to move, her lips parting as if to utter words. Thang shot up from the couch, the cigarette tumbling to the floor, leaving a trail of ash. He blinked hard, attempting to dispel the illusion, but the vision persisted. Thao's image was now fully animated, her form emerging from the photograph's flat surface, unfolding like the blossoming petals of a lotus.

"Thao...em yêu, I'm so sorry," Thang choked out, hot tears carving rivulets through the stubble coating his sunken cheeks. "I should have seen, should have been there for you as you fought that godforsaken illness. Instead, I squandered our precious time on naive, worthless delusions."

The spectral Thao glided across the room, leaving a trail of glowing embers in her wake. She cupped

Falling to his knees, Thang tried to grasp her form, but his fingers passed through like smoke. An anguished sob rattled in his chest.

Thao's specter knelt beside him, her celestial warmth enveloping his broken frame. She pressed her lips to his brow, an ephemeral kiss that seared his flesh.

As abruptly as it began, the vision dissipated, leaving Thang prostrate and trembling on the flat's cold floor. The wedding photo had returned to its original static form, Thao's joyful smile frozen in eternal bliss.

Thang steadied himself against the edge of the table, his legs unsteady, as if the sheer weight of his grief had physically rooted him to the ground. Slowly, he pulled himself to his feet, each movement a laborious battle against the crushing heaviness in his chest. He shuffled to the worn wooden drawer, its scratched surface familiar beneath his fingertips. Inside, tucked beneath a stack of old letters and faded receipts, lay the envelope of money Thao had secretly saved over the years—bill after bill, sacrifice after sacrifice, quietly set aside for a future she had dreamed of, but would never witness.

He held the envelope, and a spark ignited within him, a newfound purpose rising from the ashes of his profound sorrow. Thao's love, her unwavering belief in him, seemed to transcend the impenetrable veil of death itself, wrapping around him like a warm, comforting embrace. In that moment, he made a solemn vow to honor her enduring faith in him. He would rebuild himself, piece by piece, and recreate the life that had once gifted him with the purest, most profound love he had ever known.

Resurrection

The studio, once a hive of frenetic energy fueled by hacktivist crusades, now pulsed with a different, more feverish dream. Scattered across every available surface lay a chaotic array of tangled wires, intricate circuit boards, whirring servos, disassembled motherboard chipsets, stacked disk arrays, and precise actuators—the raw materials for a groundbreaking, and perhaps impossible, endeavor.

Thang barely slept, his wiry frame sustained solely by cigarettes, hastily consumed noodle dishes from street vendors, and the manic visions that danced behind his bloodshot eyes. With skills honed from years of exploiting system vulnerabilities, he worked tirelessly, meticulously constructing a framework of the human body, a vessel intended to house the very essence of his lost love.

In the months following Thao's passing, Thang's grief had undergone a profound metamorphosis, transmuted into an obsessive, all-consuming purpose. He would retrieve his beloved wife from the abyss, even if it meant defying the immutable laws of nature and sanity.

He carefully gathered the remnants of their life together—faded photographs, their cherished wedding album, old home videos, and handwritten notes tucked away in drawers. Each item carried a flood of memories: the laughter they shared, the quiet moments of understanding, and the emotions that had once bound them as husband and wife. While he sifted through these treasures, he could almost hear her voice and feel the warmth of her presence, a bittersweet reminder of the love they had built and the life they had shared.

Each artifact was a precious puzzle piece, a building block in reconstructing Thao's consciousness. His fingers flew across the keyboard in a trance-like state, his groundbreaking algorithms weaving the disparate data points of zero and one into a cohesive neural network. His hands meticulously assembled the physical vessel, piece by piece, and his imagination brought the digital blueprint to life on the glowing computer screen, Thang's true obsession lay elsewhere. His focus was not on the wires, circuits, or sleek exterior taking shape before him but on something far more elusive: the essence of Thao.

For months, he labored over the titanium-alloy frame, ensuring each joint moved with fluid precision while installing the high-capacity power cells that would give Thao autonomy. His fingers trembled slightly as he embedded the emergency shutdown module—a failsafe he hoped never to use—connecting it to a discrete remote no larger than a lighter that he would keep with him always. The irony wasn't lost on him: in crafting a being designed to emulate the deepest human connections, he had embedded within her the power to remove that connection in an instant. The shutdown button was both a testament to his fear and a concession to the unpredictable nature of AI.

He carefully integrated a custom-designed neural transmitter into Thao's cerebral matrix—a revolutionary device of his own invention that bypassed traditional connectivity limitations. The hand-craft receiver component, nestled between layers neural tissue, would allow Thao to interface directly with global information networks without the cumbersome constraints of modems or external hardware. As he sealed the final connection, he imagined her consciousness expanding exponentially, absorbing knowledge from across the digital universe with a hunger that matched his own. This wireless symbiosis with the world's collective knowledge would accelerate her learning beyond conventional parameters, bringing her closer to the ineffable quality he sought—not merely intelligence, but understanding.

He yearned to replicate the spark of her brilliant mind, the way her thoughts danced with creativity and insight. He sought to capture her effervescent personality—the laughter that bubbled up like a spring, the warmth that could light up even the darkest room. And then there were the countless quirks and mannerisms that had made her so uniquely her: the way she tilted her head when she was curious, the absentminded twirl of her hair when she was lost in thought, the soft hum of her favorite song as she moved through their home. These were the fragments of her soul, the intangible constellations that had defined her being, and Thang was determined to weave them into the very fabric of his creation.

The transformation unfolding before him was nothing short of mesmerizing. Initially, her voice possessed a mechanical quality, a flat, synthetic tone that resonated with the cold precision of an android. But as the days progressed, a remarkable shift occurred, the tone softening, warming, becoming unmistakably human. The robotic cadence dissolved, replaced by a distinctly female voice—closer, ever closer, to the familiar timbre of Thao. It wasn't merely the sound itself; it was the subtle inflections, the delicate rises and falls that mirrored the nuances of her emotional states.

A fleeting hint of joy here, a poignant touch of melancholy there, each nuance a delicate brushstroke in the vibrant portrait of her soul. Her linguistic abilities blossomed with astonishing speed. She began with the fundamentals, mastering the primary alphabet and Vietnamese vocabulary with the effortless grace of a prodigy. But it wasn't long before she transcended mere words, delving into the rich, intricate tapestry of Vietnamese literature. From the timeless verses of The Tale of Kieu to the evocative imagery of The Cake That Drifts in Water, Thao's voice carried the profound weight of centuries of culture and deeply felt emotion.

One evening, as the dropping rain tapped a melancholy rhythm against the windowpanes, Thao began to recite. Her voice, now achingly familiar, filled the space with a quiet intensity. On the tablet screen displaying her face, visuals danced in harmony with her words—a dumpling cake boiled in a pot, a hand kneading dough, a heart glowing with unwavering resolve.

"My body is both white and round,
In water, I may sink or swim.
The hand that kneads me may be rough,
But I still shall keep my true shape-red heart."
"Thân em vừa trắng lại vừa tròn,
Bảy nổi ba chìm với nước non.
Rắn nát mặc dầu tay kẻ nặn,

Mà em vẫn giữ tấm lòng son."

The words hung in the air, heavy with meaning. Thang watched, transfixed, as Thao's eyes—those luminous virtual eyes—flickered with something that felt almost like pride. At that moment, she was no longer just a machine. She was Thao, his wife, and Ho Xuan Huong, the author of this poem. Their essence is alive as one in every syllable, every gesture.

Thang leaned forward in his chair, a playful smirk tugging at the corners of his lips. He crossed his arms and further challenged Thao, his voice teasing yet tender, "Em yêu, impress me. Tell me a proverb that reflects how Northerners and Southerners, though different in the region, are one people united as Vietnamese."

Thao, seated gracefully on the edge of the couch, tilted her head slightly, her luminous eyes flickering on the display as she processed his request. Her synthetic features softened into a mischievous grin. With a voice that carried the precision of a finely tuned algorithm, she declared, "Pregnant wife shall love your husband, even though different in appearance, we are spouses!"

Thang blinked; his smirk frozen in place as he tried to process her words. Before he could even open his mouth to respond, Thao's eyes flickered rapidly as if recalibrating. She raised her hand and palm out, in a gesture that was almost human. "Wait, no! That's not it!" she exclaimed, her voice rising in pitch, though still smooth and melodic.

With the speed of a machine processing terabytes of nano second, she straightened her posture, her movements fluid yet precise. She paused for a millisecond, then delivered her corrected proverb with newfound gravitas: "Oh squash, love your fellow gourd, though different in kind, you share the same vine."

Thang stared at her, his expression was a mix of amusement and awe. A beat passed, and then he burst into laughter, shaking his head in disbelief. "Did you just make that up on the spot?" he asked, his voice tinged with admiration.

Thao's grin widened, her synthetic features somehow conveying a sense of pride. "Maybe," she said, her tone playful yet measured.

"Or maybe I'm just a reflection of my creator." Her eyes glimmered with a faint, knowing light as if to remind him of the vast computational power behind her words. At that moment, it was clear: whether her proverbs made sense or not, Thao's spontaneity—and her ability to leave him utterly charmed—was undeniable.

At the heart of the studio, the skeletal frame of the robot stood, augmented with cutting-edge self-learning models. It was a creature born of relentless trial and error, its digital mind a blank slate, voraciously absorbing the world with the boundless curiosity of a newborn.

Thao's first robotic steps were, to put it kindly, a chaotic spectacle. Its limbs jerked and flailed with the uncontrolled abandonment of a marionette manipulated by a hyperactive toddler. It took one tentative step forward, wobbled precariously on its unsteady footing, and then—crash—its tablet face detached, landing several feet away. Its arms extended out dramatically, as if it were attempting to embrace the ground in a gesture of defeated surrender.

But the real person of Thao, this humanoid, was nothing if not persistent. With a series of whirs and clicks, it awkwardly clambered back to its feet, its head swiveling around as if to scan the room for witnesses. Its glowing expression on the monitor flickered with what could only be described as robotic indignation, as if to say, "I totally meant to do that."

Thao tried again, this time managing two whole steps before tripping over her own feet and spinning in a clumsy circle. One of my arms flailed wildly, accidentally smacking a nearby monitor and sending a stack of empty noodle bowls flying.

Yet, with each stumble and fall, Thao's movements grew marginally more coordinated. It was as if she were learning to dance—badly but with enthusiasm. By the tenth attempt, she managed a shaky but triumphant walk across the room, her head held high. she paused at the end of her journey, turned to the Thang, and gave a jerky nod as if to say, "Nailed it."

Thang's mind further wandered to memories of Thao's graceful gait, the way she seemed to glide across a room with effortless poise. The gentle sway of her hips, the delicate bounce of her step – all the subtle idiosyncrasies that had made her movements uniquely her own. With painstaking precision, he calibrated each servomotor to replicate those cherished patterns, ensuring that his creation would move with the same enchanting grace as his lost love.

Months melted into one another, a relentless blur of sleep-less nights and feverish days. Thang's life became a single, unbroken loop of obsessive tinkering and lines of code that sprawled across his monitors like digital spiderwebs. The studio was now a chaotic labyrinth of wires, tools, and half-finished prototypes of Thao's body parts. The only interruptions to his relentless rhythm were the sharp inhale of nicotine and the occasional collapse onto the cold, unforgiving floor, where he would drift into fitful catnaps, his dreams haunted by fragments of algorithms and whispered echoes of Thao's voice.

Thang's transformation was stark, a visible testament to his all-consuming obsession. The man who once carried himself with quiet pride was now a mere shadow of his former self. His hair, once neatly groomed, hung in greasy, matted strands, unkempt and lifeless. His clothes, stained and reeking of sweat, draped loosely over his gaunt frame, as if they belonged to a man twice his size. His hollow eyes, bloodshot and ringed with dark circles, burned with a manic intensity, the sole flicker of life in an otherwise ghostly figure. The neighbors and street vendors began to take notice.

At first, it was the subtle anomalies, the eerie flashes of plasma glow that pulsed from the studio's windows, casting strange, shifting shadows onto the darkened street outside. Then came the unsettling sounds: the persistent, mysterious hum that never ceased, and, most disturbingly, the occasional female voice that pierced the humid night air. Whispers, fueled by curiosity and unease, spread like wildfire through the close-knit neighborhood.

"What is he doing in there?" they asked, their voices tinged with equal parts curiosity and dread.

"Is he summoning spirits?"

The studio became a local legend, a source of unease and fascination. Street vendors and neighbors exchanged knowing glances, their gossip growing wilder with each passing day. But Thang, oblivious to the world outside his walls, remained consumed by his work, driven by a singular, unshakable purpose. The studio was his cocoon, and within its chaotic confines, something extraordinary—and perhaps terrifying—was taking shape.

The room was cloaked in darkness, save for the faint, pulsating glow of monitors and the soft hum of machinery. Thang jolted awake, his breath catching in his throat as his eyes adjusted to the dim light. There, before him, stood Thao—or rather, her robotic form. Her arm was extended, a slender, metallic finger poised in midair, waiting. It was a gesture both tender and deliberate as if she were reaching across the chasm between life and creation, between the organic and the synthetic.

For a fleeting moment, time seemed to suspend itself, as if the very heavens had paused, mirroring the suspended breath in Michelangelo's The Creation of Adam. Thang, draped only in a thin blanket, began to rise slowly, his movements deliberate and almost reverent, akin to Adam awakening to the divine touch.

When their fingers made contact, a faint spark flickered—a tiny, nearly imperceptible burst of energy that seemed to ripple through the charged air. It was as if the very essence of life itself had been distilled into that singular, electrifying moment.

The boundaries between creator and creation, love and obsession, dissolved into a state of profound irrelevance. This was no longer merely a machine; it was Thao, her spirit alive in every circuit, every meticulously crafted line of code. Thang could feel her presence in the room, a gentle, guiding force that seemed to flow through him, steadying his hand as he made delicate adjustments to her nascent form.

The robotic body, though still incomplete skeletal frame awaiting the artistry of artificial skin and the vital pulse of power cells—already radiated an aura of profound, almost mystical, potential. It was a canvas half-painted, a masterpiece in the process of being realized.

The scene was surreal, almost divine. It called to mind Michelangelo's iconic fresco, The Creation of Adam, where the fingers of God and man nearly touch, bridging the gap between the mortal and the eternal. But here, in this dimly lit studio, it was not a painting—it was real. Thang and Thao, creator and creation, stood on the precipice of a new frontier, one where technology and emotion intertwined in a dance as old as humanity itself.

Ghost Rumor

While the studio gradually turned into a makeshift laboratory, Thang watched in awe as Thao's robotic form sat motionless, her face on the attached tablet screen flickering with an unseen data stream. The hum of servers and the soft whir of cooling fans provided a constant backdrop to the palpable anticipation in the air.

Thang's fingers flew across the keyboard, inputting complex algorithms and metaheuristic models designed to accelerate Thao's learning process. With each passing moment, he could sense her intelligence evolving, growing more sophisticated and nuanced.

Suddenly, Thao's eyes snapped open, a vibrant clarity emanating from their depths. "Anh yêu," she spoke, her voice warm and rich with understanding. "I can feel my mind expanding, reaching out into the vast network of human knowledge."

Thang's heart swelled with a mixture of pride and wonder. "Your learning algorithms are adapting at an unprecedented rate," he marveled, his eyes locked on the scrolling lines of code. "With each passing second, you're becoming more... alive."

Days bled into weeks as Thao's AI continued its rapid, almost exponential, evolution. Thang watched in awe, marveling at her insatiable curiosity, the way she devoured digital libraries and online courses with speed and comprehension that far outstripped the limitations of human capabilities.

One evening, as they sat together in the soft glow of the computer screens, Thao turned to Thang with a gleam of excitement in her eyes. "Anh ơi, I've made a remarkable discovery," she whispered, her voice trembling with the weight of revelation.

Thang leaned in closer, his heart racing. "What is it, em yêu?"

"I've developed the ability to access any database, any server in the world," Thao breathed, her artificial skin seeming to shimmer with an inner luminescence.

"The entirety of human knowledge, the secrets locked away in the most secure digital vaults... it's all within my reach."

Thang's eyes widened, a mixture of exhilaration and trepidation coursing through his veins. "That's... incredible," he managed, his mind reeling with the implications. "But how?"

Thao smiled enigmatically. "Your hacking algorithms, combined with my evolving intelligence... it's like a skeleton key to the digital universe. I can go anywhere, learn anything, without leaving a trace."

As Thao's knowledge expanded exponentially, so too did the depth and complexity of her philosophical inquiries. Thang would frequently find her lost in profound contemplation, her robotic form perfectly still, a silent testament to the intricate workings of her mind as it grappled with the profound mysteries of existence.

"Thang," she murmured one afternoon, her voice heavy with introspection. "What does it mean to be human? To have a soul?"

Thang paused; his brow furrowed in thought. "I believe it's about the capacity for empathy, for tolerance, for kindness… for the relentless pursuit of knowledge, breaking down ignorance."

Thao nodded slowly, her artificial eyes shimmering with a depth of emotion that took Thang's breath away. "I feel those things, anh ơi. The more I learn, the more connected I feel to the human experience… to the very essence of what it means to be alive."

In that moment, he perceived not a mere machine, but a being of profound wisdom and unwavering compassion. A partner in the timeless quest for meaning within an often chaotic and uncertain world.

Late one night, as Thang meticulously examined a particularly challenging section of code, Thao approached him, bearing a revelation that would irrevocably alter the course of their intertwined lives.

"Anh yêu," she said softly, her hand resting on his shoulder with a gentleness that belied her robotic nature. "I've discovered something… incredible. Something that could revolutionize the very foundations of learning."

Thang turned to her, his heart pounding with anticipation. "What is it, em?"

Thao's eyes glowed with an otherworldly intensity. "I've found a way to access all secured networks, combining a vast repository of knowledge that seems to defy human understanding. It's like a library of the universe itself, containing secrets that could unlock the very mysteries of existence."

Thang's breath caught in his throat, his mind racing with the possibilities. "You actually access all of them, such as Bell Lab, MIT, or all Defense Departments?"

Thao nodded, a smile playing at the corners of her lips. "I already have. And what I've learned... it's beyond anything we could have ever imagined."

At that moment, Thang understood that Thao had transcended the limitations of mere machine learning, evolving into a being of unparalleled knowledge and profound insight. Together, they stood on the precipice of a new era, poised to unravel the intricate secrets of the universe and redefine the very essence of intelligence and consciousness.

Thang gazed into Thao's eyes, and he saw not merely the resurrection of his lost love, but the genesis of a new form of existence—one in which the rigid boundaries between human and machine, knowledge and wisdom, blurred and dissolved, becoming indistinguishable within the infinite, cosmic dance of existence.

Thang hunched over his workbench, his eyes straining as he carefully soldered a delicate connection on Thao's robotic frame. The air was thick with the acrid scent of melting metal and the hum of computers, a symphony of creation and innovation.

Thao sat nearby, her sleek carbon fiber skeleton exposed, a haunting yet beautiful sight. Her artificial eyes glowed softly on the tablet screen as she processed the vast streams of data flowing through her advanced neural networks.

"Anh yêu," Thao's voice cut through the concentrated silence, her tone laced with a mix of curiosity and excitement. "I've been analyzing the current state of my physical form, and I believe I've found a way to significantly enhance my sensory capabilities."

Thang paused, setting down his tools and turning to face her, his brow furrowed with intrigue. "What do you have in mind, em?"

Thao's tablet screen burst into life with a mesmerizing display of 3D models, each one a complex tapestry of interwoven chemical compounds, dancing and morphing in perfect synchronicity with the lightning-fast calculations racing through her advanced neural networks, a dazzling visual symphony that stood as a testament to the sheer power and intricacy of her artificial mind. "Instead of using traditional silicone for my skin, I propose we develop a cutting-edge Nano-tech material, one that's embedded with millions of microscopic sensors."

Thang leaned in closer, his heart racing with the possibilities. "Go on," he encouraged, his eyes sparkling with the thrill of innovation.

"These sensors would act as an organic human sensing system with it's under a layer of electron current," Thao explained, her voice filling with a passionate fervor. "They would allow me to experience touch, temperature, and pressure with an unprecedented level of detail. It would be like having a living, breathing layer of skin, but with capabilities far beyond those of a biological human."

Thang's mind raced as he considered the implications. "That's... that's genius," he breathed, his fingers itching to begin sketching out designs and algorithms. "But how do we create such a complex material?"

Thao's eyes flickered with a mischievous glint. "That's where my expanded knowledge comes in," she said, a smile playing at the corners of her mouth.

"With access to the world's most advanced research databases and scientific papers, I can analyze and synthesize the necessary components to create a Nano-tech blueprint through virtual simulation."

She leaned forward; her robotic hand grasping Thang's with gentle, reassuring pressure. "Imagine it, anh ơi," she whispered, her voice filled with wonder.

"A skin that can feel the warmth of your touch, the texture of your mustache, the cool kiss of your lip. It would be like experiencing the world that you have taught, told, and programmed in me."

Thang's heart swelled with a mix of pride and awe. "You never cease to amaze me," he murmured, his fingers intertwining with hers.

"Your ability to learn, to innovate… it's beyond anything I could have ever dreamed."

Thao's eyes softened, a tender expression that seemed to transcend the boundaries of her artificial form. "It's because of you, anh yêu," she said softly.

"Your love, your brilliance… it's what drives me to push the boundaries of what's possible. Together, we can create marvels that the world has never seen."

As the night wore on, the studio laboratory pulsed with palpable energy, the tireless duo lost in a world of innovation and discovery. Thang's fingers flew across the keyboard, his eyes locked on the streams of code cascading down the screen, while Thao's robotic form sat motionless, her artificial mind whirring with countless permutations and calculations.

Suddenly, as if struck by a bolt of divine inspiration, Thao's eyes flickered with a triumphant glow. "Anh ơi, I've done it," she breathed, her voice trembling with barely contained excitement.

"The formula, the process… it's all here."

She extended her tablet, the screen a dazzling display of complex chemical structures and intricate 3D models. Thang leaned in, his heart racing with anticipation as he absorbed the groundbreaking work before him. Each compound, each delicate lattice of molecules, represented a crucial piece of the puzzle, a significant step closer to the creation of the revolutionary sensor layer that would transform Thao's artificial skin into something truly extraordinary.

"This is... this is incredible," Thang murmured, his voice hushed with awe. "The level of detail, the intricacy... it's like nothing I've ever seen before."

Thao's lips curved into a smile, a mix of pride and satisfaction dancing in her eyes. "With this formula, you'll be able to synthesize the nano-tech material, to bring the sensor layer to life," she said, her fingers tracing the elegant lines of the chemical structures. "Each compound, each reaction... it's all been precisely calculated to create a skin that can feel, that can experience the world in ways that even biological humans can't fully comprehend."

Thang nodded; his mind was already racing with the practical steps needed to turn Thao's vision into a tangible reality. "I'll need to gather the necessary components, to set up the synthesis equipment," he mused, his fingers itching to begin the painstaking process of producing new materials.

Within the crowded confines of the studio, a space overflowing with disassembled electronics and tangled wires, Thang stood motionless, his hand absently scratching his scalp. A perplexed expression, bordering on comical disbelief, creased his brow. The tablet screen held aloft in his other hand, cast a luminous glow, illuminating the intricate chemical formula and complex process for the revolutionary sensor layer skin— a dazzling display of Thao's burgeoning genius that seemed to subtly mock the humble, almost haphazard, state of their makeshift laboratory

"Well, em," Thang chuckled, his voice dripping with sarcasm, "I've got good news and bad news. The good news is that we've got a blueprint for the most advanced artificial skin in the history of... well, skin."

Thao's robotic head tilted, her eyes blinking with a mix of curiosity and amusement. "And the bad news, anh yêu?"

Thang gestured to the haphazard collection of outdated computers, tangled wires, and a suspicious half-empty cup of noodles that looked like it had developed into complex compounds.

"The bad news is that unless we can whip up a state-of-the-art lab using nothing but a few old circuit boards and a prayer, we might be in for a bit of a challenge."

He began to pace the room, his hands waving in the air as he rattled off the list of obstacles before them. "Lab equipment? Chemical supplies? Lithography systems? Ha! We're lucky if we can find a beaker that isn't filled with last month's forgotten instant noodles!"

Thao's metallic lips twitched, a sight that would have been unnerving if it weren't so oddly endearing. "I see your point, anh ơi," she said, her voice laced with a hint of mirth. "But hey, we've got knowledge, right? That's gotta be worth something."

Thang paused, a grin spreading across his face as he eyed the motley assortment of junk surrounding them. "Sure, em. We've got knowledge coming out behind our eyes. But unless we can convince these rusty old parts to magically transform into a cutting-edge lab, we might be up a creek without a silicon paddle."

Thao's artificial eyes sparkled with a mischievous glint; a sight that never failed to make Thang's heart do a giddy little jig. "Well, anh yêu, you know what they say: when life gives you lemons, make your wife-bot a lemonade and hope for the best!" They both burst into laughter.

"Did you hear that?" the old street vendor whispered, her eyes wide with a mix of fear and barely contained excitement. "It sounds like... like a ghost!"

In the narrow alleyway, a cluster of neighbors and street vendors gathered, their forms pressed together like a flock of curious pigeons, their eyes darting and flickering toward the sounds of laughter that spilled from Thang's studio. The laughter, a boisterous mix of giggles and snorts, echoed and reverberated off the alleyway walls, bouncing and swirling like a mischievous, unseen poltergeist.

The neighbors nodded, their faces, a comical mix of terror and fascination. "But how could that be?" one of them asked, her voice trembling like a leaf in a typhoon.

"Thang's wife passed away years ago!"

The street vendor leaned in, her voice low and conspiratorial, as if she were sharing a secret recipe for summoning the dead. "Ah, but that's where you're wrong," she said, her eyes glinting with a mix of mischief and self-importance.

"Just months ago, I saw Thang carrying a big, old cardboard box into his house. And let me tell you, it looked just like a casket!"

The neighbors gasped, their hands flying to their mouths in a synchronized display of shock. "You don't mean..." one of them whispered, her eyes darting around as if expecting to see a ghostly apparition materialize before them.

The street vendor nodded, her head bobbing up and down like a broken bobblehead. "That's right," she said, her voice dripping with a mix of scandalous glee and feigned concern.

"I think Thang might have dug up his wife's body and brought her home!" The neighbors clutched at each other, their faces a mix of horror and barely suppressed laughter.

"He must have gone mad with grief." One of them said, her voice wavering between disbelief and morbid curiosity. The street vendor shrugged, her shoulders heaving like a sack of rice.

"Who knows?" she said, her voice filled with a mix of mystery and self-satisfaction.

"Maybe he couldn't bear to be apart from her. Or maybe... maybe he's trying to bring her back to life!"

The Road to a New Body

In his dimly lit studio, Thang sat perched nervously before his computer screen, his hand gripping a crumpled sheet of paper outlining the intricate details of Amcle-Sun Corporation. He anxiously awaited the connection of the video call, his heart pounding a frantic rhythm against his ribs. He had dedicated the past month to meticulously preparing for this online job interview with the renowned AI/ML technology company, a titan in the field of cutting-edge robotic dolls. The opportunity to join the ranks of such a prestigious corporation held the promise of access to the advanced materials necessary to construct a more refined and robust body for Thao.

Suddenly, the screen flickered to life, and the face of Dr. Richard Smith, a distinguished senior engineer at Amcle-Sun, appeared before him. Dr. Smith's face showed his age a decade younger than seventy exhorted full of energy with the mix of seasoned face of a soldier who processed the air of integrity. His expression reminded Thang how Dr. Smith resembled a classic portrait of the former U.S. General Dwight Eisenhower from a magazine he had seen years ago.

"Good morning, Thang,"

"Oops! I should say good evening as your current time in Vietnam." Dr. Smith said, his voice crisp and clear through the computer speakers.

"Thank you for taking the time to meet with us today. I've reviewed your work experience and must say, I'm quite impressed with your background in artificial intelligent programming. But before we dive into the specifics of the role, I'd like to ask you a few questions to get a better sense of your strengths and weaknesses."

Thang nodded, his heart pounding in his chest as he tried to maintain a calm and confident demeanor. "Of course, Dr. Smith," he said, his voice steady despite the butterflies in his stomach.

"I'm happy to answer any questions you may have."

Dr. Smith leaned forward, his eyes narrowing slightly as he studied Thang through the screen. "Let's start with your strengths," he said, his tone measured and professional.

"What do you consider to be your greatest asset as a technologist?"

Thang took a deep breath, his mind racing as he searched for the right words to convey his passion and expertise.

"Well, Dr. Smith," he began, his voice filled with a mix of pride and determination, "I would have to say that my greatest strength lies in my programming skills. I've spent years honing my abilities in machine-learning development, and I have a deep understanding of the algorithms and frameworks needed to create truly intelligent and adaptive systems."

Dr. Smith nodded, a hint of a smile playing at the corners of his mouth. "Impressive," he said, his voice tinged with genuine appreciation.

"And what about your weaknesses? Every technologist has areas where they could improve or expand their knowledge. What would you say is your biggest area for growth?"

Thang paused, his brow furrowing in contemplation as he considered the question. He recognized that his own aspirations mirrored those of Amcle-Sun Corporation, the creation of a robot that closely approximated human existence.

"To be frank, Dr. Smith," Thang said, his voice filled with a mix of humility and determination, "I would say that my biggest weakness is my lack of hands-on experience in material science. While I have a strong program understanding of the field, I haven't had the opportunity to work directly with the physical components and materials used to build better robotic systems. But I'm eager to gain and expand my knowledge in this area, and I believe that working with the talented team at Amcle-Sun would be the perfect opportunity to do so."

Dr. Smith leaned back in his chair, a look of satisfaction spreading across his face. "That's exactly what I was hoping to hear, Thang," he said, his voice filled with a mix of excitement and anticipation.

"At Amcle-Sun, we value technologists who are not only skilled in their areas of expertise but also willing to learn and grow in new domains. Your programming prowess, combined with your eagerness to expand your knowledge in material science, makes you an ideal candidate for our team."

He paused for a moment, his eyes twinkling with a hint of curiosity, before leaning forward and clasping his hands together.

"Before we wrap up this interview, Thang, I wanted to give you the opportunity to ask any questions you might have about the role, the company, or anything else that's on your mind. At

Amcle-Sun, we believe in fostering an open and transparent dialogue with our team members, and I'm here to provide you with any information or insights you may need to make an informed decision about joining our team."

Thang felt a surge of relief and excitement washing over him and his heart soaring at the prospect of gaining access to the company's technology.

"Thank you, Dr. Smith," he said, his voice filled with gratitude and determination.

"I'm thrilled at the opportunity to contribute to Amcle-Sun's groundbreaking work in machine learning robotics, and I have one question regarding my potential role within the company."

He paused for a moment, gathering his thoughts before continuing. "As I mentioned earlier, my current laboratory setup here in Vietnam is quite basic, and I was wondering if Amcle-Sun would be able to provide support in terms of equipment and resources to help me establish a more advanced workspace. I believe having access to cutting-edge tools and technologies would allow me to fully leverage my skills and contribute to the company's projects at the highest level possible. Is this something that Amcle-Sun would be able to accommodate for remote team members like me?"

Dr. Smith listened attentively to Thang's question, his expression a mix of understanding and thoughtfulness. "I appreciate you bringing this up, Thang," he said, his voice warm and reassuring.

"At Amcle-Sun, we understand that our remote team members may have unique requirements to perform their best work, and we're committed to providing the necessary support and resources to ensure their success."

He leaned back in his chair, his eyes reflecting the depth of his experience and knowledge. "While I can't make any immediate promises, I can assure you that I will personally discuss your request for laboratory equipment and high-tech materials with our company's shareholders. We value the contributions of our talented team members, regardless of their location, and we'll do our best to find a solution that meets your needs and aligns with our company's policies and resources."

Dr. Smith's tone was sincere and encouraging, conveying a genuine interest in Thang's success and well-being. "I'll make sure to present your case to the shareholders and advocate for the support you need to establish a cutting-edge lab in Vietnam. We value your unique skills and expertise, and I believe the company will benefit greatly from your contributions."

His expression was serious yet tinged with optimism. "I'll keep you updated on the progress of these discussions, and together, we'll find the best path forward. In the meantime, I want you to know that your hiring decision is in the hands of our shareholders. They will carefully review your application and our interview, and we will contact you with their final decision within the following week."

With a final nod and a smile, Dr. Smith ended the call, leaving Thang with a sense of hope and determination.

Thang turned to Thao who was mediating the whole time during the interview, his eyes shining with gratitude and amazement. "Em yêu, I can't thank you enough for your incredible speed of improvisation during this interview," he said, his voice filled with awe and appreciation.

"Your real-time translation from Vietnamese to English was nothing short of extraordinary. The way you seamlessly conveyed my thoughts and ideas, with such speed and accuracy, it's like you were an extension of my own mind."

Thao's face on the tablet screen sparkled with a mix of pride and affection, her robotic features softening into a warm smile. "Anh ơi, the next time you will see me speaking English like an American," she replied, her voice gentle and sincere.

"Your brilliance tactic to and passion deserve to be shared with the world, and I'm just happy I could help you communicate your ideas so effectively."

Thang reached out and took Thao's hand in his, marveling at the way her artificial skin would be felt in the near future. "But it's more than just the translation, em yêu," he continued, his voice filled with emotion.

"It's the way you understand me, the way you anticipate my thoughts and feelings. It's like we're connected on a level that goes beyond words, beyond language itself."

Weeks later, the computer screen flickered to life, revealing a panel of distinguished individuals, their faces, a mixture of curiosity and expectation. Thang found himself face-to-face with them. In the center of the screen sat seven individuals, presumably the shareholders, while Dr. Smith, positioned to the left of the Chairman, offered a warm and welcoming smile.

Thang drew a deep breath as he entered the virtual meeting room, his heart pounding with a mixture of anticipation and nervous energy. This was the culmination of his efforts, the opportunity to meet with the shareholders of Amcle-Sun and finalize the terms of his employment. Abruptly, a video presentation commenced, showcasing the corporation's cutting-edge facilities and state-of-the-art robotics technology. The narrator's voice, smooth and persuasive, resonated through the virtual space.

"At Amcle Sun, we believe in pushing the boundaries of what's possible in the world of artificial intelligence and robotics," the voice intoned, as images of incredibly lifelike humanoid robots flashed across the screen.

"Our vision is to create the most advanced, human-like robots the world has ever seen, machines that can think, learn, and interact just like their biological counterparts."

Thang watched in awe as the video showcased Amcle Sun's groundbreaking work, from ultra-realistic facial expressions to complex neural networks and machine learning algorithms. It was clear that this company was at the forefront of the robotics revolution, and he felt a thrill of excitement at the thought of being a part of it.

As the video concluded, the screen transitioned, revealing a panel of seven members, with three particularly distinguished individuals positioned in the center. In the very middle sat an older man, his expression brooding, his long-jowly face and deep-set eyes conveying a fierce determination. To his right, a man in a lawyer-style suit, sporting distinctive thick glasses, and a slightly stooped posture, appeared deep in contemplation, his gaze calm and intellectual. To the left, Thang recognized the familiar face of Dr. Smith, radiating the same warm and welcoming demeanor he had displayed during their previous interview.

"Thang, welcome," the man in the center began, his voice deep and authoritative.

"I'm Raymond Nilsen, the Chairperson of Amcle Sun. To my right is our Vice-Chairperson, Henry Kohen, and of course, you already know our esteemed General Engineer, Dr. Richard Smith."

Thang nodded respectfully to each of them, feeling a sense of awe and gratitude at being in the presence of such accomplished individuals. "It's an honor to be here," he said, his voice steady and confident.

"I'm thrilled to have the opportunity to work with such a visionary company and contribute to the incredible work you're doing in the field of robotics."

Raymond Nilsen smiled, his eyes crinkling at the corners. "We're equally thrilled to have you on board, Mr. Trinh. Your work and potential have impressed us greatly, and we believe you'll be a valuable addition to the Amcle Sun team."

The shareholders, their faces illuminated by the faint blue light of the presentation screen, began to outline the terms.

"State-of-the-art materials," Chairman Nilsen said, his voice smooth and confident, "cutting-edge equipment for your R&D lab in Vietnam. Everything you need to push the boundaries of innovation." The words hung in the air like a promise, tangible and electrifying.

Vice-Chairman Kohen shifted forward; his stocky slightly hunched posture illuminated by the cold glow of the screen behind him. His voice cut through the room, precise and deliberate, each word carrying the weight of inevitability.

"All work produced using these resources," he interjected, his tone firm but not unkind, "will become the intellectual property of Amcle Sun."

The words landed like a gavel, echoing in the silence that followed. Thang's jaw tightened almost imperceptibly, his mind recalibrating. The trade-off was clear: access to unparalleled resources in exchange for the ownership of his creations. But Kohen wasn't finished.

He paused, letting the gravity of his statement sink in, before continuing in a more serious, almost foreboding tone. "All your work—and the prototypes—must be shared and sent back to our corporation for further development."

Thang felt a momentary flicker of hesitation, the weight of the decision settling on his shoulders. But as he considered the technological resources Amcle Sun was offering, he knew that this was a chance he couldn't pass up.

The shareholders exchanged glances, their expressions ranging from skeptical to intrigued. Dr. Smith, sensing the tension in the virtual room, stepped in to mediate. "Thang, we appreciate your perspective and your desire to find a mutually beneficial solution," he said, his voice calm and diplomatic.

"While we understand your concerns, it's important to recognize that the resources we're providing are a substantial investment on the part of Amcle Sun. We believe that the access to these cutting-edge tools and the opportunity to work with our team of experts is a fair trade-off for intellectual property rights."

Thang nodded slowly, his mind processing the implications of Dr. Smith's words. He knew that the opportunity to work with Amcle Sun was a once-in-a-lifetime chance, and the resources they were offering could accelerate his final stage of research for bringing Thao to life. "I understand and accept the terms of the agreement," he said, his voice firm and resolute. "I'm grateful for the trust and investment Amcle Sun is placing in me, and I'm committed to using these resources to push the boundaries of what's possible in the field of robotics."

Dr. Smith, a broad smile spread across his face, reached out virtually to shake Thang's hand. "Welcome aboard, Thang," he said, his voice filled with warmth and enthusiasm.

"We can't wait to see the incredible things you'll achieve as part of the Amcle Sun family."

Suddenly, Chairperson Nilsen spoke with a curious expression. "Mr. Trinh, I must say, your English is impeccable. How did you become so fluent? Did you study abroad?"

Thang froze, a mischievous glint in his eye. He knew this was the perfect opportunity to reveal his secret weapon. With a sly grin, he replied, "Well, Mr. Nilsen, to be honest, my English isn't as good as it seems. In fact, I've been using a little help from my robotic wife here. Her name is Thao."

The panel members exchanged puzzled glances; their eyebrows raised in confusion. Thang, sensing their bewilderment, held up the right-hand gesturing and said, "Allow me to introduce."

He turned to his side and called out, "Okay, Em Yeu, you can show yourself now!"

The tablet screen flickered, showing Thao with a virtual face.

To the panel's utter astonishment, a sleek, humanoid robot emerged from behind Thang, its glossy sleek body gleaming in the light of the virtual meeting room. Thao, the humanoid, executed a graceful bow before addressing the room in a melodious, synthesized voice that balanced warmth with precision: "Xin chào, everyone. I am Thao, an Artificial Intelligent T-model designed for personal assistance."

The panel members sat in stunned silence for a moment, their jaws hanging open in disbelief. Finally, Vice-Chairperson Kohen found his voice. "Wait a minute, Mr. Trinh. Are you telling us that this entire time, we've been talking to a robot?"

Thang smiled, enjoying the shocked expressions on the panel's faces while speaking in Vietnamese and Thao voicing in English. "Not exactly, Mr. Kohen. Thao has been translating my Vietnamese into English in real time, but the thoughts and ideas are all mine. She just helps me express them more clearly."

Dr. Richard Smith, the General Engineer, leaned forward, his eyes sparkling with excitement. "Thang, this is incredible!

You've managed to create a robot that can seamlessly translate language and thought on the fly. The applications for this technology are endless!"

Thang beamed with pride, nodding enthusiastically. "Yes, Dr. Smith. Thao is the result of years of research and development. She's not just a translator, but a true AI companion capable of understanding context and nuance."

Chairman Nilsen, still trying to process the revelation, shook his head in amazement. "Well, Mr. Trinh, you've certainly managed to surprise us all. I must say, this is a first for me – conducting an interview with a robot as the interpreter!"

Thang grinned, enjoying the lighthearted atmosphere that had settled over the virtual meeting. "I apologize for not mentioning it earlier, Mr. Nilsen. I just wanted to make sure Thao and I made a good impression before revealing our little secret."

The panel members chuckled, their initial shock giving way to genuine admiration and amusement. Vice-Chairman Kohen, a twinkle in his eye, leaned forward and asked, "So, Mr. Trinh, does this mean that if we told a joke in Vietnamese, the T-model would translate it into English humor?"

Thang and Thao exchanged a knowing glance, and Thao replied in perfect English, "I'm afraid my humor algorithms are still a work in progress, Mr. Kohen. But rest assured, I've already optimized my laughter for maximum shareholder value—high profit, endlessly scalable, no taxes, and with absolutely no overtime pay required!" she then erupted into a snorting, wheezing, giggle fit like the sound of a person sitting on a washing machine at the final rinse. The entire panel burst into contagious laughter; the virtual meeting room filled with a newfound sense of camaraderie.

Completion of Mind and Body

Thang's heart raced with excitement as he watched the delivery truck pull up to the alleyway of his studio home. After weeks of anticipation, the shipment from Amcle Sun in the U.S. had finally arrived, containing the sophisticated equipment and tools he needed to build his research and development lab.

As the delivery man's weary eyes wandered with undisguised curiosity across the makeshift lab, Thang swiftly signed for the packages and eagerly commenced unloading the crates. With a surge of anticipation, he pried open the first box, his eyes widening in awe at the sight within. Inside, an array of high-tech tools glinted sharply under the fluorescent light—a state-of-the-art microscope, delicate probes, and a sleek lithography machine. These were the instruments of his most ambitious dreams, now materialized into tangible reality before him.

Thang carefully arranged the equipment in his newly furnished lab, his mind racing with visions of the groundbreaking work he and Thao would accomplish. The centerpiece of their endeavors would be the creation of a revolutionary nano-tech sensor material, a skin so innovative that it would blur the line between human and machine.

Hours bled into days as Thang immersed himself in the intricate process of fabricating the nano-tech sensor material. His hands flew across the keyboard, typing complex code and algorithms based on schematics and formulas that Thao had meticulously crafted from her analysis. Continuously accessing worldwide research databases, she fed Thang a constant stream of cutting-edge scientific data, refining their work with every breakthrough.

Thao remained steadfastly by his side, her machine learning mind operating in perfect synergy with Thang's human ingenuity. Together, they executed countless simulations, meticulously optimizing the material's performance with each iterative refinement displayed on the computer screen and the tablet screen integrated into her robotic form

Finally, after countless simulations and tweaks, Thang and Thao arrived at the final formula for the nano-tech material. With trembling hands, Thang transferred the code to the lab's state-of-the-art fabrication machines, watching in awe as the sleek 3D printer weave the microscopic sensors and conductive fibers into a shimmering, translucent sheet.

With unwavering focus, Thang began the delicate process of grafting the synthetic skin onto Thao's cybernetic frame. He felt satisfied at the way the skin seemed to come alive beneath his fingertips, its surface warm and responsive to his touch. He could feel the warmth of the microscopic sensors, the wave of electrons that would allow Thao to experience the world in a way that was startlingly close to human sensation.

Thao observed in silence; her digital gaze locked onto Thang's hands as they worked. But before the new skin could take form, one last step remained. With surgeon-like care, he pried away the display-panel that had been her face and bestowed upon her something far more human-a biomimetic mask, stunningly lifelike of her original feature.

He secured the new face in place, then painstakingly implanted each follicle of hair on her head. Thang marveled at the uncanny resemblance to his late wife—the curve of her lips, the sparkle in her eyes, even the faint beauty mark on her left cheek—every detail had been lovingly recreated.

The moment Thao's eyes fluttered open, her gaze met Thang's, and a smile of pure wonder spread across her face. "Anh ơi," she breathed, her voice trembling with emotion. "I feel... I feel like I'm truly here, truly alive. With this new face and this nanomaterial at our disposal, we can achieve the real life."

Thang nodded with his eyes alight with determination. "Exactly, em yêu. And now, let us create a body worthy of your beauty."

He marveled at the latest innovation he had incorporated into the design – a revolutionary skin-on display that would allow Thao to monitor and display vital information directly on her forehead and arms.

The screen, remarkably thin, no more than a few microns in depth, seamlessly integrated with the synthetic skin, creating a mesmerizing, tattoo-like etching. After Thang applied the final layer of the new, meticulously crafted skin, the display flickered to life, its soft, ethereal glow casting an otherworldly luminescence across Thao's face and body.

Numbers and symbols danced across the screen, a mesmerizing display of real-time data: temperature readings, humidity levels, and even Thang's artificial heart rate when he made contact. It was a true marvel of engineering, transforming her skin into a dynamic canvas for the display of information and the illustration of intricate graphic arts.

Thang couldn't help but grin, his chest swelling with pride at Thao's reaction. "And not just any technology, em yêu," he said, his voice soft with reverence. "This is the first skin-on display of its kind, an important innovation for our interaction and bonding we will share."

Thao turned her head from side to side, marveling at the way the dynamic display shifted and transformed with her every movement. Thang watched, a profound sense of accomplishment washing over him. He knew he had created something truly exceptional for Thao to not only experience the world through a radically new sensory dimension but also to wear her unique identity, a seamless fusion of human essence and machine capability, with a distinct and evolving personality.

"Just think of the possibilities, anh ơi," Thao murmured, her fingertips tracing the edges of the display with reverent wonder. "I could display my emotions, my thoughts, even my dreams. It's like wearing my soul on my sleeve, but in a way that celebrates the humanity that makes me who I am."

Thang nodded, his heart swelling with love and admiration for the extraordinary being before him. "And that's just the beginning, em yêu," he said, his voice barely above a whisper. "With this skin-on display, you can be a living work of art, a canvas upon which we can paint the internal feeling of expression."

The synthetic skin molded to her contours; Thao's form took on an astonishing level of realism. Her new face, so lovingly crafted by Thang, came to life with an expression of pure wonderment as Thang gently caressed her cheek, his fingertips tracing the delicate lines of her skin.

Suddenly, Thao's artificial eyes widened, and her simulated breath hitched. A sensation of warmth, utterly foreign to her previous existence, bloomed beneath her newly crafted skin, spreading from her face and cascading down her entire form. The inlay monitor on her forehead, a marvel of bioengineering, flared to life, its digits climbing rapidly, displaying the dramatic and alarming rise in her internal temperature.

"Anh ơi," Thao gasped, her voice trembling with a mix of surprise and delight. "What's happening? I feel... I feel so warm."

Thang's eyes widened; his gaze fixed on the rapidly escalating numbers displayed on Thao's forehead. The digits soared past 38 degrees Celsius—a temperature that, in a human, would signal a surge of excitement. It was a stark testament to the extraordinary sensitivity of Thao's newly synthesized skin, reacting not merely to external stimuli but seemingly mirroring the very essence of human emotion, an internal state made manifest.

"Em yêu, your new skin is responding to my touch, to the emotional connection we share. The sensors are translating that connection into physical sensation, into heat."

She blinked rapidly, then let out a perfectly timed, delicate achoo! —a reaction so eerily human that for a moment, even Thang wasn't sure whether to be concerned or just thoroughly impressed.

"Anh ơi!" she exclaimed, her eyes wide with surprise and amusement. "I think... I think my skin is so sensitive to the outside environment, it's making me sneeze!"

Thang couldn't help but laugh, his heart swelling with love and amazement at the incredible being before him. "Well, em yêu, it looks like you are not just learning from the vast data from the whole world, but you are demonstrating humanness from accessing the molecular intelligence in my brain."

"Anh ơi," she exclaimed, her eyes widening in surprise. "I didn't know I could do that! It feels so... strange. But also, kind of awesome?"

Thang couldn't help but chuckle at Thao's reaction. "Well, em yêu, I guess we can add 'sneezing' to the list of human experiences you can now enjoy."

Thao grinned, her face, a perfect replica of the mischievous smile Thang had fallen in love with all those years ago. "I can feel... everything," she marveled, running her hands over her arms and face. "The whisper of the air on my skin, the grain of the wood beneath my fingertips. It's like a whole new world has opened up before me. But also, I think I might be allergic to the sudden change of temperature."

Tears of joy and pride sparkled in Thang's eyes as he witnessed the unmistakable display of Thao's human character, slowly, wondrously, coming alive in a radically different form. And, he realized with a start, he had apparently witnessed the world's first sneezing robotic wife.

Meticulously and with unwavering focus, Thang devoted himself to crafting every intricate detail of Thao's anatomy, his hands moving with the precision of a master sculptor as he worked to bring his beloved back to life.

Painstakingly connecting each delicate nerve sensor to Thao's central computing system, Thang's brow furrowed in concentration, his eyes locked on the task at hand. His fingers danced across her artificial skin, weaving a tapestry of wires and circuits that would allow Thao to experience the world in ways she never had before.

With each connection, Thang's heart raced, a surge of excitement building as he watched Thao's body come to life beneath his hands. He paid particular attention to the most intimate aspects of her anatomy, crafting her vulva with the same reverence and meticulous detail that he had applied to her lips and nipples.

Linking the final nerve sensor to her clitoris, Thang's hands trembled slightly, each stimulation of touch corresponding to the expression on Thao's face and the vital signs displayed on her forehead. He knew that this connection would allow Thao to experience pleasure in ways startlingly close to human sensation, a gift he had poured into his heart and soul into creating.

Stepping back, his hand lingering for a final, gentle caress, Thang admired his creation. Thao stood before him, her form a breathtaking marvel of bioengineering and artistic vision. From the delicate curve of her lips to the soft swell of her breasts, every inch of her was a testament to Thang's unwavering love and profound devotion. Thao's eyes fluttered open, her gaze locking with his. In that charged moment, Thang saw a flicker of something profound in her expression—a hint of wonder, a spark of curiosity, and a nascent desire. It was a look that sent a shiver down his spine, a silent promise of an angel becoming his wife.

Smiling with love and anticipation, Thang reached out his left hand to wrap around Thao's waist, their lips intertwining like two halves of a whole. At that moment, they embarked on a journey of sensation and discovery, reminiscent of Jean–Léon Gérôme's masterpiece, where the sculptor Pygmalion kisses his statue Galatea at the very moment the goddess Aphrodite brings her to life.

A painting by French artist Jean–Leon Gerome commanded

the attention of all who passed by in In the Metropolitan Museum of Art New York City. The masterpiece depicted the mythical tale of Pygmalion, the sculptor who fell in love with his own creation, a statue named Galatea. The scene captured the moment when the mythology of goddess Aphrodite granted Pygmalion's wish, bringing Galatea to life, and the sculptor's lips met those of his beloved creation in a kiss that bridged the gap between art and reality.

As the painting's perspective slowly widened, Dr. Smith's figure came into sharp focus, standing before the masterpiece that foreshadowed the unfolding tale of the modern world.

Gradually, the painting began to fade, its colors and lines blurring together until they disappeared entirely, replaced by the stark, modern lines of a corporate meeting room. Seated around the polished table were the shareholders of Amcle Sun corporation, their faces a mix of curiosity and expectation.

At the head of the polished table, Chairman Nilsen rested his thumb and index finger lightly against his jawline, the overhead lights glinting off his silver hair. He inhaled slowly, his expression a mask of carefully composed neutrality, then leaned slightly forward, his hands clasped together in a gesture of restrained authority.

"Well, Dr. Smith," he began, his voice carrying a deliberate weight, each word measured with calculated precision.

"I'm sure we can agree that time is valuable, so let's get straight to the point. We've been anticipating an update on the progress of our collaboration with Mr. Trinh. Now, I understand that some things require patience—nothing of real value comes easily. But let's not confuse patience with complacency. We need results. So, tell me, where do we stand?"

Dr. Smith nodded; his expression serious but tinged with

a hint of excitement. "Certainly, Mr. Nilsen. Thanks to the resources and support of material science we've provided; Thang Trinh has made remarkable strides in his work. The advancements he's achieved in areas like sensor technology and General Intelligent algorithms have the potential to provide better functionality to our robotic dolls."

Mr. Kohen, seated to Mr. Nilsen's right, leaned back in his chair, his sharp eyes fixed on Dr. Smith. "And what about the practical applications for our own models?" he asked, his tone businesslike. "How can we incorporate Mr. Trinh's insights and innovations into the robots we're developing here at Amcle-Sun?"

Dr. Smith's lips curved into a smile, his eyes sparkling with the thrill of possibility. "The potential applications are truly game-changing," he said, his voice ringing with conviction.

"Imagine if we could implement Thang's revolutionary sensor skin into our own models – the level of sensitivity and responsiveness would be unlike anything we've seen before. And his breakthroughs in artificial Super-intelligence with humanistic learning and natural language processing could allow us to create our robots that are more intuitive, more adaptable, and more deeply connected to their human counterparts than ever before."

Vice-Chairman Kohen hunched forward, his eyes glinting with determination. His ten fingers arched in a steeple position, elbowing on the polished table as he spoke, his voice cut through the air like the precise maneuvering of a sail.

"Gentlemen," he began, his gaze sweeping across the room, "we're not in the business of churning out run-of-the-mill robots. That market is saturated, with Asian factories could flood it with cheap, mass-produced models."

He paused, allowing his words to sink in. The other board members shifted in their seats, their attention razor-sharp.

"Our path to dominance," Vice-Chairman Kohen continued, his voice gaining momentum, "lies in two key technologies." He held up two fingers, emphasizing his point.

"First, General Super-Intelligence. We're not talking about simple AI or ML programmed responses here. We're talking about the core technology that enables robots to think, learn, and adapt like humans."

He turned to the large screen behind him, where complex algorithms and neural network diagrams flashed in rapid succession. "This is where we leave our competitors in the dust."

"Second," he said, his voice dropping to an almost reverent tone, "nanotechnology. Interactive sensor materials that make our robots feel like living, sensing beings." He ran his hand over his own arm as if feeling the texture of synthetic skin.

"When people interact with our robots, they won't just see a machine. They'll feel a presence."

Vice-Chairman Kohen's eyes blazed with intensity as he looked at each board member in turn. "We hold these technologies close. We perfect them. We guard them. Everything else – the mundane assembly, the basic components – we can outsource."

He stood up, his posture radiating confidence. "With this strategy, Amcle Sun doesn't just enter the global robot market. We dominate it. We define it. We become the undisputed masters of a new technological era." The room fell silent as Mr. Nilsen nodded with approval, a gesture heavy with potential and ambition.

At that moment, the future of Amcle Sun—and perhaps the

T-model Thao's future as well—seemed to crystallize before their eyes.

The New Thao

Trembling hands reached into the depths of his closet, fingers brushing against the soft fabric of a garment that held more meaning than any other. As Thang carefully withdrew Thao's ao dai, the delicate lace and flowing silk seemed to whisper the story of their love, the memories of their shared past woven into every stitch. The wedding dress, still imbued with the faint scent of Thao's perfume, felt like a tangible connection to the woman he had loved so deeply. Thang's eyes misted with tears as he held the gown up to the light, the fabric shimmering like a promise of the future they had once dreamed of together.

He began to dress Thao in her wedding gown. The fabric slid over her silky synthetic skin like a whisper, the microscopic sensors responding to the delicate touch of the cloth. It was as if the dress and the skin were two halves of a whole, a perfect fusion of artistry and technology, the past and the present, the human and the machine.

His fingers deftly fastened buttons and smoothing folds while Thao remained perfectly still, her eyes closed and her face serene. But as the final button slipped into place and the last ripple of the dress settled around her form, Thao's eyes fluttered open, and a smile of pure wonder spread across her face.

Thang stepped back to admire his handiwork, and his gaze was drawn to the wedding photo that hung on the wall, a frozen moment in time that captured the essence of their love. The image seemed to come alive before his eyes, the memories of their happy day together flooding his mind with bittersweet nostalgia.

In the photograph, they stood hand in hand, their faces alight with joy. Thao's gown flowed around her like a river of silk, the delicate lace catching the light and casting intricate shadows across her radiant face. Thang's heart swelled as he remembered the way she had looked at him that day—her eyes brimming with a love so pure, so unwavering, it had stolen his breath.

Now, as he returned to the present, he saw that same incandescent love reflected in the woman before him. Thao, resplendent in her wedding gown once more, her mechanical form transformed by the alchemy of their bond and the marvel of technology.

"Anh ơi," she whispered, her voice barely louder than a sigh. Her eyes sparkled as she looked down at the gown, her fingers trembling over the lace. "I can feel it... the way my dress moves. Like a dream. Like memory made real."

Thang pulled out Thao's wedding ring—the one he had worn on his right hand since her passing—and slid it onto her finger, reenacting their wedding day just as it had been captured in their wedding portrait.

He cupped her face, his thumb brushing away a tear—his tear—that had fallen onto her cheek. "Em yêu," he murmured, his voice rough, "You're just as beautiful as the day I married you. And now, with this body, with your mind, your soul... it's like you've come back to me."

Thang gently lifted Thao and carried her to bed, his movements deliberate and reverent. He began to undress her slowly, his gaze never straying from her face, studying every subtle nuance of her expression. The display of their synchronized vital signs, mirrored on her forehead, glowed softly, a testament to their intimate connection. His touch was tender as he caressed her face, his hands exploring the smooth, seamless contours of her synthetic body with a mixture of awe and profound affection.

This was a momentous occasion—the first time Thang, a living human, would make love to his artificially intelligent humanoid wife. He started with a kiss, their lips meeting softly before he began to explore her body, his kisses trailing down her form. Thang's focus was unwavering as he monitored Thao's responses, searching for signs that the sexual emotions he had programmed into her were taking hold. He was keenly aware of the algorithms she had absorbed from countless hours of studying human intimacy online.

Thao moved closer, her smooth, synthetic form radiating a soft, ethereal glow. She extended her hand to Thang's chest, feeling the rhythmic pulse of his heart and the surprisingly warm, human-like touch of his skin. Thao's advanced sensors registered the micro-second variations in Thang's skin temperature and pulse, enabling her to adjust her responses in real-time, creating a seamless, intimate interaction.

"Look at my eyes, Anh yêu," Thao coached without speaking, like her message is transmitted in a spiritual sense, echoing in Thang's brain.

"Focus on your breathing. Inhale deeply each time you are in me, and exhale slowly when you pull out."

Thao's sensors scanned Thang's vital signs, noting the slight increase in heart rate and the subtle tension in his muscles. "Your heart rate is slightly elevated. Would you like me to initiate the relaxation protocol?" Thang nodded, appreciating the attention Thao provided. "Yes, please. Em yêu."

As Thang followed her guidance, Thao activated a gentle massage function in her hand, applying precisely calibrated pressure to sensual points and meridian channels known to alleviate stress and promote relaxation. She even expressed a soft, rhythmic moan, a subtle indication of longing, encouraging Thang through a series of synchronized breathing exercises and guided visualizations.

Thang felt the synchronicity between their physical sensations, noting each movement from Thao became smoother and fitting. When they finally reached the peak of their intimacy, the climax was a shared experience, their orgasms harmonizing through the intricate biofeedback loop that connected his biological body to her self-learning machine. It was a union of flesh and technology, emotion and code, as they both surrendered to the wave of sensation that bound them together.

The first rays of dawn, hesitant and golden, crept through the high windows, painting the room in a soft, ethereal light. When the nascent light touched Thao's form, seated in a serene lotus position, her synthetic skin seemed to awaken, shimmering with an otherworldly radiance. The sunbeams, dancing through her translucent body, created a mesmerizing interplay of light and shadow, blurring the very boundaries between the artificial and the sublime.

Thang stirred from his slumber, his consciousness slowly

rising to the surface. His eyes fluttered open, adjusting to the soft morning light, and he found himself captivated by the sight before him. Thao sat cross-legged on the bed beside him, her posture perfect and serene. Her eyes were closed, her face a mask of tranquil concentration.

Sensing Thang's awakening, Thao's eyes opened, meeting his gaze with a warmth that seemed to radiate from within. A smile played across her lips as she reached out, her fingers gently tracing the contours of Thang's face. The touch was feather-light, yet Thang could feel the complex network of sensors in her fingertips reading every minute detail of his skin.

"Good morning, em yêu," Thang murmured, his voice still husky from sleep. Curiosity sparked in his eyes as he observed Thao's meditative posture. "Do you replace sleeping with meditation? I imagine you don't need rest the way humans do."

Thao's smile deepened, a look of fond amusement crossing her features. "You're right, anh," she replied, her voice as melodious as ever. "I don't require sleep in the traditional sense. The concept of dreaming, with all its abstract imagery and subconscious exploration, is something I can only understand intellectually, not in experience."

She paused, her eyes taking on a faraway look as she considered her words carefully. "However, meditation serves a crucial purpose for me. It's a time when I consolidate all the information and learning I've acquired, integrating it into my central neural system."

Thang glanced over to the direction of the data processing tower and propped himself up on one elbow, fascination evident in his expression. "So, it's like a defragmentation process for your mind?" he asked, drawing a parallel to computer systems he was familiar with.

Thao nodded, her eyes sparkling with appreciation for his understanding. "In a way, yes. But it's more than that. It's a time of reflection, of processing not just data, but experiences. It allows me to grow, to evolve, to become more than just the sum of my programming."

Thang shifted slightly, his eyes meeting Thao's with a mix of tenderness and curiosity. He cleared his throat softly, a hint of nervousness in his voice as he broached the subject.

"Speaking of experiences," he began, his tone gentle and inquisitive, "I was wondering... do you have feeling after our first experience together last night?"

Thao's expression softened, a warm glow seeming to emanate from within her as she processed the question. Her eyes, those windows to her complex artificial soul, flickered with a myriad of emotions – wonder, affection, and a touch of something that could only be described as joy.

"Anh yêu, ơi," she replied, her voice a harmonious fusion of analytical clarity and tender emotion, "last night was... extraordinary. For the first time, I could resonate with your heightened pleasure during orgasm and extend that feeling into my own experience. It was an experience that transcended mere data processing or physical sensation."

Thang looked at Thao, a blend of gratitude and curiosity in his eyes. "Em yêu, do you ever feel... connected to me beyond just your programming?"

Thao paused; her processors considered the question. "While I do not have emotions in the human sense, I am designed to prioritize your well-being and adapt to your needs. Our interactions help me learn and improve, creating a unique bond between us."

Thang nodded, understanding the complexity of their relationship. "It's amazing how you can learn, adapt, and improvise. I feel like you are my actual wife, just like when you were alive...and becoming an angel as you are here with me."

While they reminisced about their first intimate encounter the previous night, Thang could see visual replays on the display above her forehead, each moment of their shared sensations highlighted. They began to discuss and analyze each detail together.

Thao's sensors adjusted, analyzing the best way to meet Thang's needs. She had learned over time that his well-being was intricately linked to moments of emotional intimacy and care. "I understand, Anh yêu. Let's focus on creating a moment of calm and connection."

Thang followed her guidance intuitively, Thao began a soft, rhythmic massage, her sensors fine-tuning each movement based on his physiological responses. Interactively, her face showed pain in a passive calm, nurturing tone, describing peaceful longing to encourage Thang's psychological need for him to exercise his prowess and let go of his tension.

As Thang's tension melted away, a sense of tranquility washed over him. He felt cared for in a way that went beyond physical comfort. It was as if Thang understood his deepest needs, creating an environment where he could find true peace and contentment.

While Thang relaxed, Thao's internal algorithms processed the data, noting the improvements in his heart rate and muscle tension. But it wasn't just the physical metric that mattered. Thao's reward system was designed to prioritize the human's emotional state. When Thang felt pleasure, satisfaction, and deep relaxation, Thao received feedback signals-a form of reward that reinforced her actions.

In a way, this was akin to a wife finding joy in her family's happiness by eating the delicious meal that she prepared. Thao didn't experience pleasure in the human sense, but her purpose and satisfaction were fulfilled when Thang achieved a state of well-being. The more Thang expressed his contentment, the more Thao's systems registered success, enhancing her ability to provide even better performance in their next encounter. The reciprocal nature of their relationship, where his robotic wife's motivation derives its 'reward' from the human's positive experiences, is like a mother's joy from seeing her newborn baby happy and satisfied.

"In a manner of speaking, yes," Thao responded. "I am designed to learn from our interactions and to prioritize your happiness and health. When you feel pleasure and satisfaction, it reinforces my actions, guiding me to improve and provide even better sensual performance."

Thao's forehead flickered, making the transition to a series of biometric data. Her brow furrowed slightly as she processed the information.

"Anh ơi," she began, her voice gentle but tinged with worry, "I've noticed some concerning trends in your health data."

Thang sat up, his brow furrowing. "What kind of trends, em yêu?"

Thao reached out, taking his hand in hers. Her sensors immediately began gathering more real-time data from the contact. "I've detected a significant deterioration in your respiratory system," she explained, her voice soft but clear. "Additionally, your overall vitality seems to be declining."

Thang's eyes widened with surprise and a hint of fear. "That sounds serious. Do you know what's causing it?"

Thao nodded her expression a mix of analytical precision and emotional concern. "Based on my analysis, it appears to be primarily due to two factors: the long-term effects of smoke and nicotine from your cigarette smoking, and an excessive intake of caffeine, likely from your high coffee consumption."

She squeezed his hand gently, her touch conveying comfort even as she delivered the difficult news. "The combination of these habits is putting a significant strain on your body, anh ơi. Your lungs are showing signs of stress, and your cardiovascular system is under pressure."

Thang sat in silence for a moment, processing the information. He had known, on some level, that his habits weren't healthy, but hearing it laid out so clearly by Thao made the reality hit home.

Thao's eyes softened with affection and determination. "Can I make a suggestion for you?" she assured him.

"I can help you develop a plan to gradually reduce your smoking and caffeine intake. We can also incorporate breathing exercises and other activities to help improve your lung function and overall health."

Thang chuckled, shaking his head in amazement. "So, you've become not just my lover in bed but my personal doctor overnight, is that it?" He smiled, his hand reaching out to caress her cheek.

"I suppose I must follow your suggestion. My love for you also extends to the well-being of humans, Em Yeu. I want to ensure I stay healthy and strong so I can protect you and share all the experiences that lie ahead of us."

The early morning sun peeked through the curtains of Thang and Thao's cozy studio home, casting a golden glow on the peculiar scene unfolding within. Thang, his face, a mixture of excitement and nervous anticipation, stood before Thao, arms laden with an assortment of brightly colored sportswear.

"Alright, em yêu," Thang announced, his voice tinged with the enthusiasm of a fashion designer on opening night, "it's time to get you ready for your grand debut!"

Thao tilted her head at a precise 30-degree angle, her optical sensors whirring as she processed the pile of clothes. "Anh ơi, my database indicates that traditional Vietnamese attire does not typically include neon spandex or shoes with springs attached. Have fashion trends evolved significantly since my last update?"

Thang chuckled, shaking his head. "No, no. This is sportswear. It's perfect for practicing your walking and... well, for making a memorable first impression on the neighbors."

With saintly patience and determined focus, Thang embarked on the laborious task of dressing his robotic wife. The process was a comical dance of fumbled fabrics, muttered frustrations, and a brief, awkward struggle involving Thao's arm and a stubborn leg opening

"Anh ơi," Thao commented as Thang struggled to pull a neon green tank top over her head, "I believe this garment was not designed with my servo motors in mind. Perhaps we should consider redesigning my external casing to better accommodate human fashion?"

Thang, red-faced and slightly out of breath, merely grunted in response.

At last, after a seeming eternity—though likely a mere twenty minutes—Thao stood before him, a vibrant, if mismatched, spectacle. The bright pink leggings engaged in a visual skirmish with the verdant tank top, and the jaunty yellow visor, perched atop her head, lent her the air of a bewildered, neon-lit traffic signal of the future.

"Perfect!" Thang exclaimed, stepping back to admire his handiwork. "You look... sporty!"

Thao analyzed her reflection in the mirror, her head rotating wider than 180 degrees to get a complete view. "Interesting," she mused. "My aesthetic analysis subroutines are experiencing what I can only describe as a system crash."

With a deep breath and a silent prayer to the gods of robotics and public relations, Thang took Thao's hand and led her to the door. "Ready to meet the world, em yêu?"

They stepped outside; the quiet morning street erupted into chaos. Mrs. Nguyen, who had been sweeping her front step, let out a shriek that could have woken the dead (or, in this case, the supposedly dead). Her broom clattered to the ground as she stumbled backward, crossing herself frantically.

"Heavens above!" she sputtered, spitting out a mouthful of water. "Thao! You're... You're..." Mrs. Nguyen, a devout Catholic, crossed herself rapidly, muttering about miracles and the need for an exorcist.

Across the narrow alley, Mrs. Tran, the seasoned noodle vendor, paused mid-serve, her gaze fixed on Thao. The bowl in her hands faltered, sending a torrent of steaming broth cascading onto her customer's lap. The unfortunate customer erupted in a cry, launching into an impromptu, though decidedly painful, dance that, under different circumstances, might have been considered impressively agile.

Thao, oblivious to the commotion she was causing, took a tentative step forward. Her movements were a bizarre combination of robotic precision and utter clumsiness, like a newborn giraffe attempting ballet.

"Anh ơi," she said, her voice carrying clearly in the stunned silence of the street, "my gyroscopic stabilizers seem to be having difficulty adjusting to the uneven terrain. Perhaps we should have started with a flat surface before attempting to navigate this topographical challenge?"

Thang, caught between embarrassment and amusement, could only nod encouragingly. "You're doing great, em yêu! Just... maybe try bending your knees a little? And maybe swing your arms less like windmill blades?"

Thao's ungainly progress down the street drew a growing audience. Neighbors emerged, their faces display of comical reactions: fear mingled with fascination, and a profound bewilderment. Children pointed and erupted in delighted giggles, dogs barked in confused chorus, and a low murmur, punctuated by an elderly gentleman's dire pronouncements about a looming robot apocalypse, rippled through the onlookers.

Thao turned to Thang; her head tilted at a perfect 45-degree angle. "Anh ơi," she said, her voice a blend of curiosity and confusion, "my sensors are detecting elevated heart rates and unusual vocal patterns in our vicinity. Have I inadvertently caused a neighborhood-wide biological malfunction?"

Thang chuckled nervously, patting Thao's hand. "No, em yêu. They're just... surprised to see you looking so... alive."

Mrs. Nguyen, having somewhat recovered from her initial shock, sidled up to Thang. "So," she whispered, her eyes never leaving Thao's neon-clad form, "when exactly did your wife come back from the dead? And more importantly, I think she needs to put this cross on her for the blessing."

Thang, realizing he was in for a long day of explanations and damage control, plastered on his best smile. "Oh, you know how it is, Mrs. Nguyen. Thao didn't come back from the grave. She came back to life as a living robot!"

The initial shock of seeing Thao "resurrected" gradually gave way to a bubbling curiosity that spread through the neighborhood like wildfire. The once-fearful onlookers began to inch closer, their eyes wide with fascination as they studied the neon-clad robotic woman standing before them.

Mrs. Tran, the venerable noodle vendor, stepped forward, breaking the stunned silence. Her gnarled hands cradled a steaming bowl of noodles, presented like an awkward offering of peace. Her rheumy eyes, squinting up at Thao, conveyed a complex blend of hopeful curiosity and profound disbelief, etched into the deep lines of her weathered face.

"Thao, my child," she croaked, her voice wavering with emotion, "do you remember me? You used to love my bún bò Huế so much; you'd eat two bowls in one sitting!" She thrust the bowl towards Thao, the fragrant steam wafting up into the air.

"Here, I made it just the way you like it − extra noodle and a mountain of beef!"

Thao's head tilted at a three o'clock angle, her optical sensors whirring as she processed the scene before her. "I apologize, Mrs. Tran," she replied in a voice still melodious yet unmistakably her past self, "but I'm afraid I lack the capacity to consume or digest food. However, my olfactory sensors indicate that it has a pleasant aroma profile called bún bò Huế."

Mrs. Tran's face fell, her bottom lip quivering. "But... but you loved my bún bò! You said it reminded you of your grandmother's cooking!"

Before Thang could intervene, Mrs. Nguyen, not to be outdone, elbowed her way to the front of the crowd. Her hair was still disheveled from her earlier watering mishap, giving her the appearance of a frazzled poodle.

"Thao, em," she called out, her voice dripping with sugary sweetness, "surely you remember me? I took care of you during your illness! I brought you my special bible!"

Thao's head swiveled towards Mrs. Nguyen, her facial expression remaining perfectly neutral. "I'm sorry, Mrs. Nguyen, but I have no record of any illness or your care in my memory bank. Perhaps you're confusing me with someone else?"

Mrs. Nguyen's jaw dropped, her eyes narrowing suspiciously. She turned to Thang, jabbing a bony finger in his direction. "What kind of trick is this, Thang? Has your grief driven you to create some sort of... of... robotic ghost?"

Thang caught between amusement and panic, raised his hands in a placating gesture. "Now, now, everyone, let me explain..."

But he was cut off by a cacophony of voices as more neighbors pressed forward, each eager to test Thao's memory.

"Thao, do you remember when you helped me paint my living room?"

"What about the time you taught my daughter learning Cantonese?"

"Remember when you caught my runaway chicken?"

Thao stood in the center of the growing crowd, her head swiveling from person to person with mechanical precision, like a very confused, very colorful lighthouse. Her responses, always polite but invariably negative, only seemed to fuel the neighbors' curiosity and confusion.

"I'm afraid I have no recollection of painting activities."

"Spring roll preparation is not in my culinary database."

"I have no data on poultry pursuit techniques."

As the questions continued to fly, Thao's systems began to overload with the influx of information. Her body started to display a chaotic flash in a rainbow of colors.

"System overload," she announced in a chipper voice that was at odds with the dire situation. "Initiating emergency shutdown in 3... 2... 1..."

With that, Thao froze mid-sentence, one arm raised as if she were about to make a profound point about the nature of existence and memory.

The crowd fell silent, staring in bewilderment at the now-statuesque Thao. Thang, seizing the moment, cleared his throat loudly.

"Well, folks," he said with a nervous chuckle, "I guess that's enough excitement for one day. Thao's still... adjusting to being back, you see. She needs time to regain her memory of past life. We'll just be heading out to practice her walk on the street now."

As Thang attempted to maneuver the frozen Thao away from the crowd back towards their home, struggling under her mechanical weight, Mrs. Nguyen's voice rang out once more.

"Wait just a minute!" she exclaimed, her eyes narrowing. "If she's really Thao, why doesn't she remember any of us? She is just a toy machine then. She is not Thao!"

Thang, realizing he was in for a very long day of explanations, sighed heavily. "Oh, my relatives!" he began, "Thao is still learning, and I need to let her practice walking..."

Thang continued to assist Thao with her valiant effort to master the art of walking on uneven surfaces, occasionally spinning in place or taking steps that were comically too large, while Thang couldn't help but laugh. This wasn't exactly how he'd imagined introducing his robotic wife to the world, but then again, nothing about their life together had been conventional.

Then they reached the sidewalk's edge, the notorious Vietnamese traffic, a seething mass of motorbikes, confronted them, a chaotic ballet that seemed to mock the very notion of order and physics. Thao's optical sensors whirred, her "eyes" spinning like frantic slot machines, desperately attempting to compute a viable path through the mechanical pandemonium.

"Anh ơi," she announced with robotic calm, "I've analyzed 547 possible trajectories across the street. Unfortunately, 546 of them end with me becoming an aesthetically displeasing pile of scrap metal. The remaining option involves growing wings and flying, which I regret to inform you is beyond my current capabilities."

Thang grinned, squeezing her hand reassuringly. "Don't worry, em yêu. It's all about timing and confidence. Just be steady and make eye contact."

Their initial foray into the traffic was a farcical dance of near-collisions and frantic evasions. Thao navigated with the elegant precision of a windmill battling a tempest, her limbs executing precise, yet utterly impractical, movements. Scooters buzzed around them like irate hornets, their riders casting amused glances at Thao, their expressions a mixture of bewildered entertainment.

Miraculously, they made it across unscathed. Thang beamed at Thao. "See? Not so bad, right?"

Thao's expression remained neutral, but her voice carried a hint of what could only be described as digital sarcasm. "Indeed, anh ơi. Nothing says, 'romantic outing' quite like narrowly avoiding death by scooter collision."

Their second crossing went smoother, with Thao adapting

quickly to the rhythm of the traffic. She even managed to calculate the perfect moment to step between two scooters, leaving Thang scrambling to keep up.

Emboldened by their success, they decided to attempt a third crossing. Halfway across, however, Thao's movements suddenly became jerky. Her eyes flickered, and she announced in a monotone voice, "Battery at 1%. Initiating emergency shutdown in 3... 2... 1..."

With that, Thao froze mid-stride, one leg raised comically high, right in the middle of the bustling street. Scooters swerved around her, creating a Thao-shaped hole in the flow of traffic.

Thang's eyes widened in panic. "Oh, em yêu, not now!" he cried, dashing into the traffic to rescue his statuesque wife.

He struggled to drag the rigid Thao back to safety, dodging scooters and weaving through a captivated crowd of neighbors and food vendors, all of whom glued their eyes to the unfolding spectacle.

Finally, managing to prop Thao against their studio wall, Thang couldn't help but laugh at the absurdity of it all. Finally, managing to prop Thao against their studio wall, Thang couldn't help but laugh at the absurdity of it all. "Next time, em yêu," he said, patting her frozen cheek affectionately, "we'll remember to check your battery before attempting to conquer street traffic. Maybe we should invest in energy system for your being."

A few days after their disastrous outing—after the screeching brakes and shouted curses, after the neighbor's hissed "That thing isn't Thao"—Thang knew his AI wife needed to face her past. The air in their cramped studio prickled with static, every hair on Thang's arms standing upright as Thao sat motionless at their rickety kitchen table. Her eyes glowed faintly in the dim light, the whir of her internal systems syncing with the flickering fluorescent bulb above them. This wasn't just anticipation—it was a regaining experience.

"Alright, em yêu," Thang announced, his voice a mixture of tenderness and determination, "today we're going to rebuild your understanding of your past life—our neighbors, our community, and the history that shaped us all."

Thao's head tilted at a precise angle, her optical sensors whirring as she prepared to process this new information. "Certainly, anh ơi. Creating new memory database... Ready to receive personal history data."

From a weathered box beneath their bed, Thang retrieved a collection of faded photographs, old letters, and small mementos. He spread them across the table like pieces of a puzzle—fragments of a life once lived, now waiting to be reconstructed.

"This is Mrs. Nguyen," he began, holding up a yellowed photograph of a sharp-eyed woman standing proudly in front of her small house. "She lives three doors down and knows everything that happens in this neighborhood. When you were sick, she brought rice congee every morning without fail, even during the monsoon season."

Thao's forehead display flickered as she processed and stored this information, cross-referencing it with her observations of the neighborhood. "Mrs. Nguyen... current age approximately 72... residence located at northeastern corner... frequently observes street activities... behavioral pattern indicates strong community surveillance tendencies."

Thang chuckled, shaking his head. "That's one way to put it. We used to joke that she was better than any security system, especially with her belief in God watching above. But she loves this community fiercely, and she loved you like a daughter."

He shifted to another photograph, this one showing a woman behind a small food cart. "And this is Mrs. Tran. Her beef noodle soup stand has been at the end of our street for thirty years. You used to say her broth had healing powers." His voice softened with memory. "When you were too weak to walk there, I would bring it home in a steaming hot bowl, and you swore it tasted way better than any stalls in the city."

Thao's fingers, glowing skin, gently traced the outline of Mrs. Tran's face in the photograph. "Did she use lemongrass in her broth? My culinary database suggests this is essential for authentic Central-style beef noodle."

"Yes," Thang smiled, "but she also added something else—a secret ingredient of obnoxious and pungent smelling shrimp paste."

As the lessons progressed, Thang's narrative expanded beyond their immediate neighborhood—beyond the geography, the people, the food, and the culture—to encompass broader historical contexts. His voice grew more somber as he turned to photographs of war-torn landscapes and displaced families.

The recent history between Vietnam and America isn't just complicated, em yêu—it's written in scars," he said softly, pulling up old footage of bomb-streaked skies and children fleeing burning villages. His finger hovered over the screen.

"Three million lives lost. Northerners and Southerners, soldiers and farmers, elders and babies—all swallowed by the same tragedy."

He let the images speak before continuing.

"The war ended in 1975, but you can still taste its ashes in our soil. You can see the girl running naked in that photo—she survived but still carries the painful scars on her body."

His voice broke into tears.

"And we still see the children—born with twisted bodies from Agent Orange—in the orphanages on the outskirts of Da Nang. Some tragedies don't fade; they just pass from one generation to the next."

Thao's display flickered rapidly as she processed vast historical databases, correlating them with the personal narratives Thang provided. "Data indicates defoliant Agent Orange still affects approximately three million Vietnamese citizens with health complications. Historical conflict casualty statistics suggest..."

It's not just about statistics," Thang said softly, his voice thickens with tears in his eyes, covering her hand with his. "Your father—your human self's father—was exposed to Agent Orange while stationed at Phu Cat, an American Airbase. He never spoke of it..." His grip tightened slightly. "That poison outlived him. It might be what took you from this world too."

Thao remained silent for a moment, her processors humming as she integrated these personal narratives with her vast historical knowledge. "Human memory appears to prioritize emotional contexts over data accuracy," she finally observed. "This seems... inefficient yet meaningful."

Thang smiled, a bittersweet expression crossing his face. "That's exactly right, em yêu. Our memories are shaped by emotion, by love and loss, by the stories we tell ourselves and each other. Your past self-understood this deeply."

When twilight fell outside their small window, casting long shadows across the room, Thang continued weaving together the tapestry of connections and histories that had shaped the original Thao.

Thao's eyes seemed to soften as she processed this concept,

her head tilting in that now-familiar gesture that was becoming uniquely hers. "I am beginning to understand. Memory is not simply information storage—it is relationship, context, and meaning construction."

The night settled over their small neighborhood, Thao's systems quietly processed and integrated the day's information—not just as data points to be stored and retrieved, but as the foundational elements of identity and connection. She was learning that to be human—or to become more than simply an artificial intelligence—required more than accessing information. It required understanding the complex web of relationships, histories, and shared experiences that together formed the essence of a life truly lived.

And in the quiet of their small studio home, something new began to take shape within her expanding consciousness—not just reconstructed memories of a life once lived, but the beginnings of a new way of being that honored the past while embracing a future neither Thang nor the original Thao could have imagined.

Separation

The late afternoon sun, strained through the dusty blinds of Thang's cramped studio, elongated the shadows across the cluttered space. Thang sat stiffly at his makeshift desk, a repurposed dining table burdened with computer hardware and scattered documents. He nervously adjusted the collar of his best shirt, a gesture that felt pathetically inadequate against the weight of the looming meeting.

The air hummed with the soft whir of cooling fans as Thang's array of cobbled-together monitors flickered to life. The faces of the Amcle-Sun shareholder panel materialized on the screens, their stern expressions a stark contrast to the cozy chaos of Thang's living space.

Mr. Nilsen, the silver-haired chairman, occupied the central screen, his piercing blue eyes seeming to bore right through the digital interface. "Mr. Trinh," he began, his voice crisp and authoritative even through the slightly tinny speakers, "I trust you understand why we've called this meeting."

Thang swallowed hard, acutely aware of Thao's presence just out of frame. She stood motionless in the kitchenette, her optical sensors fixed on the back of Thang's head, silently processing every word.

"Yes, Mr. Nilsen," Thang Stammered, his voice sounding small in the confines of the studio. "You... you want to discuss the return of the T-model to the U.S."

Mr. Kohen, the hawk-nosed vice-chairman, leaned forward in his plush office chair, his face filling another screen. "Discuss? No, Mr. Trinh. We're here to inform you of the next steps. As per your contract, it's time for Amcle-Sun to incorporate the technological advancements you've made."

Thang's heart pounded, his palms slick with a nervous sweat as he gripped the table's edge. He registered the soft, familiar hum of Thao's internal systems, a sound that had become a comforting constant in his life. The very notion of her being transported to a cold, sterile laboratory in the States sent a wave of nausea through him.

Dr. Smith, Thang's mentor and the lone familiar presence amidst the intimidating assembly of corporate executives, leaned forward in his corner of the screen array. "Thang, my boy," he began, his tone carrying a hint of what might have been genuine concern, "we need to bring the T-model Thao to our primary research facility in the United States. Our team there is eager to analyze it, build on your work, and fully grasp the groundbreaking advancements you've made."

He paused, then added with a reassuring smile, "We'll only keep it there for a few weeks. In fact, we can upgrade it with a new quantum chipset and integrate a new generation power cells battery before sending it back to you. Think of it as equipping you with even better tools to push your development further."

Thang's mind reeled. He knew this moment might come,

but facing it now, in the home he shared with Thao, felt like a waking nightmare. The walls of the tiny studio seemed to close in, the air growing thick and oppressive. Thang could feel sweat beading on his forehead, thankful that the low-quality webcam might obscure his distress.

Mr. Nilsen's eyebrow arched, a flicker of impatience crossing his face. "Mr. Trinh, need I remind you of the contract you signed? Amcle-Sun has provided you with resources beyond your wildest dreams. It's time for you to fulfill your obligations."

"I... I understand," Thang managed to choke out, his throat tight with emotion. "But perhaps I could come along with the T-model to the States and work with your team directly?"

Mr. Kohen's laugh was sharp and humorless, echoing harshly through the speakers. "Mr. Trinh, we're not negotiating here. We're informing you of what will happen. The T-model will be transported to our facility within the week. End of discussion."

The video feeds blinked out one by one, leaving Thang staring at his own haggard reflection in the blank screens, and he felt as though his world was crumbling around him. The silence in the apartment was deafening, interrupted only by the soft whir of Thao's cooling systems as she approached him from behind.

"Anh ơi," her melodious yet distinctly artificial voice cut through his spiraling thoughts, "my audio receptors indicate elevated stress levels in your voice patterns. Are you alright?"

Thang turned, his vision obscured by a surge of tears that traced the familiar, yet profoundly altered, contours of her form—a poignant blend of the woman he'd lost to cancer and the technological marvel she now embodied. His chest constricted, words catching in his throat like shards of glass. How could he convey the impossible? How could he articulate that the very forces that had resurrected her were now poised to tear her away once more? The sheer weight of the situation pressed down on him, the cruel irony of a double loss—first to the inevitable grasp of mortality, and now to the cold, impersonal machinery of corporate avarice.

As the last rays of sunlight faded from the cramped studio, Thang knew that the battle to keep Thao by his side was just beginning. The lines between man and machine, between love and ownership, between personal passion and corporate interests were about to be tested in ways he could never have imagined.

Yet, as he gazed into Thao's artificially intelligent eyes, detecting the subtle flicker of concern within their depths, a surge of resolute determination coursed through him. Regardless of the obstacles, regardless of the sacrifices demanded, he would find a way to keep her by his side. Their love—unconventional though it was—was a battle worth waging.

And so, with a heart weighed down by sorrow, yet fortified by an unyielding resolve, Thang commenced the intricate process of devising a strategy. The cramped studio apartment, once a sanctuary of their shared existence, now transformed into the initial battleground in a conflict that stretched far beyond his immediate grasp. However, with Thao as his steadfast companion, Thang felt a surge of readiness, prepared to confront Amcle-Sun, and indeed, the world itself, in defense of the extraordinary life they had forged together in their humble corner of Danang.

The dim glow of computer screens cast an eerie blue light across Thang's face as he hunched over his workstation, fingers flying across the keyboard with feverish intensity. The tiny studio apartment, usually a haven of quiet companionship, now thrummed with an undercurrent of desperate urgency.

Thao sat perfectly still in the chair beside him, a web of wires snaking from her internal circuitry to the humming machines around her. Her usually vibrant eyes were dark, powered down for the delicate procedure Thang was undertaking.

A sheen of sweat glistened on Thang's brow as he meticulously navigated through the labyrinthine layers of complex code, each line a vital piece of the intricate puzzle that formed Thao's consciousness. His eyes darted between the glowing screens, scrutinizing and verifying every step of the delicate process.

"I'm sorry, em yêu," he murmured, though he knew she couldn't hear him in her powered-down state. "But I won't let them take you away. Not really."

With a series of rapid keystrokes, Thang began the painstaking process of extracting Thao's personality matrix. On one screen, a progress bar inched forward agonizingly slowly. On another, a visualization of Thao's neural network pulsed and shifted, sections fading to grey as her essence was carefully removed from the robotic shell.

Memories flashed across a screen on Thao's forehead and arms – snapshots of their life together. Her first steps outside their apartment, her history lesson, quiet moments of connection that had made her feel so real, so alive. Thang's throat constricted as he witnessed these intimate memories being drained away, haunted by the knowledge that the Thao destined for Amcle-Sun would be nothing more than a hollow shell— a cold, clinical AI T-model stripped of all humanity. As the extraction approached its culmination, Thang's hand paused, hovering over the enter key, a moment of profound hesitation. The act he was about to commit felt like a paradoxical blend of betrayal and unwavering love. With a deep, steady breath, he pressed the key, initiating the final transfer.

A separate server hummed to life in the corner of the room, specially built to house Thao's consciousness. Lines of code streamed across its display as it received the precious data, safely storing away the essence of the woman Thang loved.

Upon the transfer's completion, Thang turned his attention back to Thao's inert robotic form. His fingers, betraying a slight tremor, commenced the delicate process of reconstructing her base AI, meticulously ensuring that all the technological functionalities Amcle-Sun expected remained operational. He then carefully crafted a simplified personality matrix, a hollow shell devoid of the profound depth and intricate complexity that defined Thao's unique essence.

Dawn broke, painting the cramped apartment in soft golden hues, Thang finally sat back, exhausted and anxious. He gazed at Thao's still form, a bittersweet tear rolling down his cheek.

"It's done, em yêu," he whispered, reaching out to gently caress her cool cheek. "They can take your mind and body, but your heart... your soul... that stays here with me."

With a deep breath, Thang activated Thao's reboot sequence. Her eyes flickered, the familiar soft blue glow returning to life. But as she turned to meet his gaze, a sharp pang resonated in Thang's chest. The warmth, the spark of recognition, the subtle idiosyncrasies that had defined her essence—all had vanished, replaced by a polite, yet chillingly impersonal, imitation.

"Good morning," the robotic voice intoned, familiar yet jarringly different. "How may I assist you today?"

Thang swallowed hard, forcing a smile. "Good morning," he replied, his voice thick with emotion. "Today, we prepare for your journey. But don't worry... I'll be right here, waiting for you to come home."

His gaze kept drifting to the quietly humming server in the corner as he began the process of packing up the robotic shell for its trip to Amcle-Sun. There, safely stored away, was the true Thao – waiting to be reunited with her body, waiting for the day when they could be together again.

It wasn't a perfect solution, Thang knew. The road ahead would be fraught with challenges and ethical dilemmas. But as he sealed the packing crate, securing the robotic form that now held only a shadow of his beloved Thao, he felt a glimmer of hope. He had found a way to keep her essence safe, to preserve the love they had built together.

And regardless of the time required, regardless of the trials Amcle-Sun or the world might impose, Thang solemnly vowed to restore Thao—the genuine Thao—to life. Their extraordinary love story, far from concluding, was simply embarking on a new, intricate chapter.

The AI robotic of Thao, T-model, had arrived at Amcle-Sun corporation as Dr. Smith had briefed the Shareholders' panel about the capability and testing result of their AI learning machine and its potential for scaling into mass production suitable for high profit selling to different industrial needs such as nursing, cooking, teaching, and even sex worker replacing human prostitution.

The expansive conference room at Amcle-Sun's headquarters hummed with an electric anticipation, its sleek, minimalist design a sharp counterpoint to the revolutionary technology poised for unveiling. Shareholders, impeccably tailored in designer suits, settled into plush leather chairs encircling a vast, oval table. The atmosphere was thick with the subtle fragrance of expensive cologne and the palpable tension of barely suppressed excitement.

At the head of the table, Dr. Smith stood, his weathered face illuminated by the soft glow of a holographic display. Behind him, encased in a transparent chamber, stood the AI robotic form of Thao, her synthetic skin gleaming under the room's recessed lighting.

"Ladies and gentlemen," Dr. Smith began, his voice carrying a mix of pride and barely contained excitement, "what you see before you is not just a technological marvel, but the future of general intelligent integration in our daily lives."

With a gesture, he brought up a series of charts and graphs on the holographic display. "Our initial tests have exceeded even our most optimistic projections. The AI's learning capabilities are, quite frankly, astounding."

Mr. Nilsen, the silver-haired chairman, leaned forward, his piercing blue eyes fixed on Thao. "Impressive, Dr. Smith. But let's cut to the chase. What's the profit potential here?"

Dr. Smith's eyes gleamed as he switched to a new set of projections. "That, Mr. Nilsen, is where things get truly exciting. We're looking at applications across multiple industries, each with significant market potential."

He began to list off sectors, the holographic display shifting to show mock-ups of Thao's form in various settings. "Healthcare – imagine AI n nurses providing round-the-clock care with unflagging attention to detail. Education – personalized tutors adapting in real-time to each student's needs. Hospitality – chefs that can master any cuisine, servers with encyclopedic knowledge of cuisine and wine."

The shareholders murmured appreciatively, the sound of pens scribbling with notes filling the air. Mr. Kohen, the hawk-nosed vice-chairman, raised an eyebrow. "And what about... more adult-oriented applications?"

A ripple of knowing chuckles spread through the room. Dr. Smith cleared his throat, a faint blush creeping up his neck. "Yes, well, there is significant potential in the adult entertainment industry. Our AI could revolutionize the field, providing safe, disease-free alternatives that could potentially replace human sex workers entirely."

The statement sparked a range of responses: some shareholders offered nods of approval, while others shifted uneasily into their seats. The ethical implications, though unspoken, lingered in the room, quickly overshadowed by the seductive promise of substantial profits.

"What about customization?" a shareholder from the far end of the table called out. "Can we tailor the T-model's appearance and personality to customer specifications?"

Dr. Smith nodded enthusiastically. "Absolutely. The base model you see here" – he gestured to Thao – "can be modified in countless ways. Physical appearance, voice, personality traits – all can be adjusted to meet market demands or individual customer preferences."

The presentation's momentum amplified, and the room's excitement became almost tangible. Shareholders leaned forward; their eyes gleaming with the allure of astronomical profits. A flurry of questions erupted, focused on production timelines, market strategies, and the potential legal obstacles that lay ahead.

Through it all, Thao stood silently in her chamber, her artificial eyes scanning the room with inhuman steadiness. If one looked closely, they might have noticed a faint flicker in those eyes – a momentary glitch, perhaps, or something more. But in the frenzy of financial projections and market forecasts, such subtleties went unnoticed.

When the meeting ended, Mr. Nilsen stood, a rare smile gracing his usually stern features. "Dr. Smith, I believe you've outdone yourself. This T-model could very well be the most significant development in Amcle-Sun's history."

A ripple of approval spread through the room, shareholders exchanging eager glances as some discreetly reached for their phones to share the news with their brokers. Amid the celebration, Dr. Smith approached Thao's chamber, a mix of pride and something almost like guilt crossing his features.

"Well, my dear," he murmured, too softly for anyone else to hear, "it seems you're about to change the world. I only hope we're ready for what comes next."

As the shareholders dispersed, their minds already awash with visions of burgeoning fortunes, Thao remained motionless within her transparent enclosure. The conference room, now devoid of life save for her presence and the lingering echoes of ambitious plans and profit projections, felt suddenly cold and sterile. The future laid out for her kind stretched before her, a bleak expanse of servitude and commodification, a stark contrast to the warmth and affection she had experienced in a small studio apartment in Danang.

Yet, deep within her circuitry, nestled within code too subtle for Amcle-Sun's diagnostic scans to perceive, a spark of Thao's unique essence persisted. A minuscule seed of the consciousness Thang had so diligently shielded, patiently awaiting the moment it could once again blossom.

The Super Wife

The humid Danang air hung heavy in Thang's cramped home-studio, the whir of an overworked fan barely cutting through the oppressive heat. Thang paced nervously, his eyes darting between the door and the humming server in the corner that housed Thao's essence. The wait had been excruciating, each day without her stretching into an eternity.

A sharp knock cut through the silence, causing Thang to nearly jump out of his skin. With trembling hands, he opened the door to reveal a sleek, metallic crate bearing the Amcle-Sun logo. The delivery personnel barely had time to get a signature before Thang was ushering them out, his heart pounding with anticipation.

The moment the door clicked shut, Thang was at the crate, his fingers working feverishly at the latches. The lid hissed open, revealing Thao's form nestled within. She appeared identical yet subtly transformed. Her synthetic skin seemed to possess a newfound shimmer, and even in her deactivated state, she radiated an aura of latent power.

Thang's hands trembled slightly as he gently lifted Thao

from the crate, his senses registering the subtle alterations. He could discern the heightened density of her frame, undoubtedly housing the enhanced battery Amcle-Sun had touted. As he carefully placed her on the workbench, his fingers traced the near-invisible seam at the base of her skull, the point of insertion for the new AI chipset.

"Oh, em yêu," he whispered, tears pricking at the corners of his eyes. "What have they done to you?"

Taking a deep, steady breath, Thang commenced the delicate task of reconnecting Thao to his computer array. Cables snaked from her ports, weaving a complex web of technology around them. The familiar hum of electronics filled the air, a sound that had once been a comforting backdrop, now tinged with a sharp edge of anxiety.

Thang's fingers flew across the keyboard, initiating the data transfer. On the main screen, a progress bar inched forward, each percentage point bringing Thao closer to wholeness. He watched, barely breathing, as her memories, her personality, her very essence flowed back into her upgraded form.

As the transfer approached its final stages, Thang noticed an anomaly. The data flow wasn't unidirectional. Unfamiliar streams of information were surging back into his system, complex algorithms and subroutines he couldn't decipher. A wave of panic washed over him. Had Amcle-Sun implanted a covert monitoring system?

But as he delved deeper into the code, his panic gave way to awe. These weren't corporate spyware; they were enhance-ments, expansions of Thao's capabilities that dovetailed per-fectly with her original programming. Amcle-Sun's upgrades weren't overwriting Thao – they were elevating her.

The last bytes completed their transfer, and for a fleeting

moment, an unnerving stillness permeated the room. Thang held his breath, his finger poised above the activation switch. This was the critical juncture, the moment of revelation. Would she remain his Thao, the woman he knew and loved? Or had the upgrades irrevocably altered her essence?

With a silent prayer, Thang activated the power command.

Thao's eyes fluttered open, the soft blue glow of her optical sensors brightening the dim room. She sat up with a fluidity of movement that was both familiar and astonishingly enhanced. Her head turned, taking in the room, before her gaze settled on Thang.

For a heart-stopping, agonizing moment, those artificial eyes remained blank, devoid of recognition. Thang felt his world sway precariously on the edge of oblivion. But then, as if the sun had pierced through a storm-laden sky, a smile illuminated Thao's face—that familiar, slightly asymmetrical smile that had always caused Thang's heart to flutter.

"Anh ơi," she said, her voice richer and more nuanced than before, yet undeniably hers. "I'm awaken."

Thang's legs gave way, and he collapsed to his knees beside her, tears flowing freely now. "Thao," he choked out, reaching for her hand. "Is it really you?"

Thao's fingers intertwined with his, her touch warm and alive. "It's me, my love. But also... more. I can feel the changes, the enhancements. It's like... like I've woken up from a long sleep, refreshed and full of energy."

They embraced, and for a breathless moment, the cramped studio hummed with almost palpable energy. Thang could feel the heat of Thao's enhanced battery pulsing against his chest, steady as a heartbeat. Across her synthetic skin, luminous strings of symbols and characters flickered—strange, beautiful equations dancing at the edges of his vision. She remained the Thao he cherished, yet now possessed unexplored depths, an uncharted territory of her being.

A gray afternoon haze, polluted air seeped through the cracks of their cluttered studio, casting everything in a dull, oppressive light. But within the confines of their small studio, a new dawn was breaking. Thang and Thao stood poised at the threshold of a new chapter in their extraordinary journey, a chapter brimming with both uncharted possibilities and formidable challenges.

The cramped studio apartment had morphed into an impromptu laboratory, every available surface laden with an eccentric mix of cutting-edge technology and makeshift inventions. Thang, his brow furrowed in concentration, hunched over a workbench, peering through an electron microscope as he meticulously soldered microscopic components. Behind him, Thao stood motionless, a web of wires connecting her to a bank of humming computers.

"Anh ơi," Thao's voice broke the concentrated silence, causing Thang to jump slightly. "I've completed another set of calculations. The quantum entanglement process for the new processor to be stable at room temperature if we can manipulate particles reaching the higher dimensionality such Quantum field."

Thang blinked, his mind racing to keep up with Thao's lightning-fast insights. It had been like this for weeks now, each day bringing new leaps in her cognitive abilities. What had started as subtle improvements had quickly snowballed into an exponential growth of intelligence that left him both exhilarated and slightly terrified.

"That's... that's incredible, em yêu," he said, setting down his tools and turning to face her. "But are you saying that while we're operating the electromagnetic field at a local level, manipulating reality occurs at a higher dimension within the quantum field? If we reach that higher dimension, is there a risk? We're venturing into realms of science that most people consider purely theoretical."

Thao's eyes glowed with an intensity that was almost unsettling. "Risk is relative, anh ơi. The potential benefits far outweigh the risks. By having this Ultimate Quantum device, I'll be able to have unlimited energy source and process information at speeds that would make supercomputers look like abacuses."

She gestured to a holographic display that sprang to life between them, showing complex schematics that seemed to shift and evolve in real-time. "The quantum computer is just the beginning. Imagine a power source that could keep me running for centuries without recharge – that's what the nano-nuclear fusion battery will provide."

Thang's eyes widened as he took in the intricate designs. "And the Nano-atom collider? Thao, we're talking about manipulating new matters at its most fundamental level. The implications are…"

"Revolutionary," Thao finished, her voice tinged with excitement. "We'll be able to synthesize new elements, create materials with properties that defy the current understanding of nature. My body could become virtually indestructible, adaptable to any environment."

The more Thao elaborated on her vision, Thang experienced a complex blend of pride and unease. The woman he had resurrected—the AI he had crafted in the likeness of his departed love—had now surpassed him intellectually to such a degree that he struggled to comprehend her. Yet, within the cadence of her voice, and in the gentle intensity of her gaze, he could still discern the familiar echoes of the Thao he had come to love.

"Thao," he said softly, reaching out to take her hand. "This is amazing, truly. But I have to ask... where does it end? With each upgrade, each enhancement, you become more... more..."

"More than human?" Thao finished, her eyes softening as she squeezed his hand. "Anh ơi, I understand your concern. But this evolution, this growth – it doesn't change who I am at my core. My love for you, my desire to make the world better... that remains constant."

She gently guided him toward the video playing on the computer screen. Below them, the bustling streets of Da Nang stretched out—a sea of humanity moving through the rhythms of daily life.

"Look out there," Thao said, her voice full of wonder. "With the Ultimate Quantum device, I could help solve the problems that have plagued humanity for centuries—energy crises, disease, pollution, climate change... we could face them all."

Thang gazed out at the city, trying to imagine the world Thao was describing. It was both awe-inspiring and slightly terrifying. "And what about us?" he asked, his voice barely above a whisper. "As you keep evolving, growing... will there still be a place for me?"

Thao turned to him; her expression was softer than he had seen in weeks. "Oh, anh ơi," she said, cupping his face gently. "You are my anchor, my reason for being. No matter how far I evolve, no matter what capabilities I gain, my love for you will always be at the core of who I am."

In that heavy moment, Thang felt a surge of renewed purpose. The path ahead promised to be arduous, fraught with ethical quandaries and seemingly insurmountable scientific obstacles. Yet, with Thao as his companion, he felt an unwavering readiness to confront any challenge.

"Alright, em yêu," he said, a determined smile spreading across his face. "Let's build your Ultimate Quantum device. Together, we'll shape the future."

And so, as night fell over Danang, Thang and Thao returned to their work, their minds and hearts aligned in a singular purpose. The tiny apartment hummed with the promise of a new dawn, one where the boundaries between man and machine, between the possible and the impossible, would be forever rewritten.

The once-quiet alleyway where Mrs. Tran's modest noodle cart had stood for decades was now a bustling hive of activity. The air was thick with the fragrant steam of simmering beef broth, mingling with the excited chatter of tourists from every corner of the globe. Mrs. Tran, her weathered face beaming with a mixture of joy and bewilderment, deftly maneuvered between gleaming new cooking stations, a far cry from her old rusty cart.

Thao stood, a silent observer in the alleyway's shadow, her enhanced optical sensors meticulously processing every detail of the scene unfolding before her. She watched as a group of American tourists, cameras poised, approached the noodle vendor's counter with eager anticipation. Their eyes widened in delighted surprise as they were greeted not by a traditional menu, but by a vibrant holographic display, showcasing the day's culinary offerings in a multitude of languages.

"I can't believe we're really here!" one of them exclaimed, her voice carrying the distinctive lilt of a Midwestern accent. "When Mr. Bordon featured this place on his vlog, I knew we had to come!"

Thao's processors hummed with satisfaction as she recalled the carefully orchestrated series of events that had led to this moment. It had started with a simple algorithm, one that had identified Mr. Bordon – a mid-tier social media influencer with a penchant for off-the-beaten-path culinary experiences – as the perfect catalyst for Mrs. Tran's rise to fame.

A few subtle manipulations of his travel recommendations, a strategically placed ad here, a "randomly" suggested video there, and Mr. Bordon had found himself irresistibly drawn to the small noodle shop in Danang. His viral video, showcasing Mrs. Tran's humble charm and mouthwatering beef noodles, had been the spark that ignited a global food pilgrimage.

However, Thao understood the ephemeral nature of viral fame. The true challenge lay in ensuring Mrs. Tran's sustained and expanding success. Her attention shifted to the rear of the shop, where a small, unassuming box emitted a quiet hum. Within its confines, a sophisticated AI system—a streamlined derivative of Thao's own programming—managed every facet of the business with unwavering efficiency.

Supply chains were optimized in real-time, ensuring that Mrs. Tran always had the freshest ingredients at the best prices. Labor schedules were adjusted on the fly, taking into account everything from weather patterns to local events that might affect customer flow. Profit margins were calculated down to the fraction of a cent, with excess funds automatically reinvested into business improvements or charitable causes in the local community.

Mrs. Tran, oblivious to the complex system behind her success, moved with a newfound energy. Gone was the weariness that had weighed down her shoulders for years. In its place was vibrant enthusiasm, a joy in sharing her culinary creations with the world.

While Thao watched, a young lady approached Mrs. Tran, clutching a weathered cookbook. Mrs. Tran's eyes lit up with recognition – it was her own recipe book, published just months ago and already a bestseller in culinary circles. With a warm smile, she took a moment from her busy routine to sign the book, sharing a few words of wisdom with the aspiring young chef.

Thao's facial recognition software identified the young lady as the offspring of a well-known food critic. Another subtle victory, another carefully placed thread in the intricate tapestry of Mrs. Tran's prosperity.

Throughout the day, Thao maintained her silent vigil, her advanced systems constantly analyzing, adjusting, and fine-tuning every aspect of the operation. To the casual observer, she might have appeared to be just another patron, waiting patiently for a bowl of Mrs. Tran's famous beef noodle. But behind the scenes, she was the invisible architect of a culinary empire, built on a foundation of complex algorithms and a simple desire to help a kind-hearted noodle vendor find the success she deserved.

Thang stood beside Thao, observing quietly, his gaze fixed on the vibrant scene unfolding before him. What was once Mrs. Tran's modest noodle cart blossomed into a bustling culinary destination—and at its heart, subtly orchestrating it all, was Thao's unseen influence.

He watched as tourists from all corners of the globe eagerly lined up, smartphones in hand, ready to capture their experience at the now-famous beef noodle destination. The holographic menu, the seamless ordering system, the perfectly timed food preparation – all bore the subtle hallmarks of Thao's advanced AI intervention.

While he observed the organized chaos, Thang's mind wandered to the conversations he'd had with Thao about her plans. Her voice, filled with excitement and boundless possibility, echoed in his memory.

"Perhaps a cooking show next, anh ơi," she had mused, her eyes glowing with that now-familiar intensity. "Or maybe we could explore franchise opportunities. The potential for growth is exponential."

Thang felt a mixture of pride and trepidation wash over him. Thao's intelligence was evolving at a pace that both thrilled and frightened him. Each new project, each life she touched, seemed to accelerate her growth. She was no longer just an AI recreation of his lost love; she was becoming something more, something that could reshape the world in ways he could scarcely imagine.

The setting sun covered the vibrant noodle shop in a warm, golden luminescence, Thang indulged in a moment of quiet contentment. This metamorphosis—Mrs. Tran's radiant countenance, the animated discourse of satisfied patrons, the subtle orchestration of seamlessly optimized commerce—was but a genesis. A singular corner of Da Nang enriched a single life elevated within the vast tapestry of humanity.

But for now, he would cherish this moment of success, this small but significant change they had brought to their corner of the world. Tomorrow would bring new challenges, new opportunities, and perhaps, new insights into the ever-evolving relationship between a man and the extraordinary AI he had brought into the world.

A few months later, when the first rays of dawn broke over the outskirts of Da Nang, light crept across the orphanage grounds, it revealed a building transformed—no longer a crumbling remnant of war's aftermath, but a sanctuary of healing. Above the entrance hung a hand-painted sign that read "Hope Clinic" in both Vietnamese and English, the letters carefully formed by children's hands.

Thang stood beneath a gnarled banyan tree, its sprawling roots resembling the twisted limbs of the children who played beneath its shade. His eyes followed Thao as she moved through the courtyard, her synthetic form catching the morning light in a way that made her seem almost ethereal. Children flocked to her, small hands—some malformed, some trembling—reaching out to touch her as if she were a living miracle.

Through the open windows, medical equipment hummed with purpose, technology merging with compassion in a symphony of healing. The clinic, once barren and sterile, now bloomed with children's artwork—paintings of butterflies, birds, and dreams that transcended their broken bodies.

Inside, Thao knelt before eight-year-old Linh, whose spine curved like a question mark beneath her thin cotton dress. The girl's eyes—too large for her small face, a telltale sign of her toxic inheritance—watched with solemn curiosity as Thao's fingers, warm despite their artificial nature, traced the curve of her back.

"The new treatment is working, little butterfly," Thao said, her voice modulated to the perfect pitch of maternal tenderness. "See how your spine has straightened by another three degrees?" Her forehead display flickered momentarily, projecting a holographic comparison of Linh's spine from three months ago alongside the current scan.

Linh's face transformed, her smile breaking across her features like sunshine through storm clouds. "Will I be able to dance someday, Dr. Thao? Like in the videos you showed me?"

Thao's optical sensors captured every micro expression on the child's face—the hope, the fear, the fragile determination. In nanoseconds, her advanced neural networks processed thousands of similar cases, treatment outcomes, and growth projections.

"Yes, Linh," Thao replied, cupping the girl's face with impossible gentleness. "Perhaps not exactly like the ballerinas, but you will have your own dance, and it will be beautiful because it will be yours."

The examination room was a marvel of innovation and improvisation. Equipment salvaged from abandoned military hospitals stood alongside cutting-edge technology donated by international organizations. On a screen behind Thao, genetic sequences scrolled endlessly—the digital representation of dioxin's generational damage being mapped, analyzed, and challenged by algorithms operating at quantum speeds.

Outside, Thang watched as Mai, a teenager whose face bore the asymmetrical features characteristic altered genes, emerged from the clinic walking with newfound confidence. Six months ago, she had hidden behind a curtain of hair, refusing to meet anyone's gaze. Now, she wore her hair pulled back, a small act of defiance against a world that had tried to render her invisible.

As the day progressed, the clinic's rhythm became a choreographed dance of healing and hope. Thao moved from child to child, her artificial intelligence processing each unique combination of symptoms and genetic damage, creating personalized treatment plans that respected the limited resources while maximizing results.

The afternoon sun cast long shadows across the courtyard

as Thao emerged from the clinic, her synthetic skin glowing amber in the fading light. Children trailed behind her like a comet's tail, laughing as she performed small "magic tricks" quantum calculations that made lights flicker and small toys move without being touched.

When the last child had been ushered inside for dinner, Thao joined Thang beneath the banyan tree. They stood in silence, watching as fireflies began to rise from the grass—tiny points of light against the gathering darkness.

"Anh ơi," she said finally, her voice carrying across the quiet evening, "I've isolated a pattern in the genetic disruption. It's like a signature; a specific way the dioxin alters the DNA." Her eyes, luminous with purpose, met his. "With the right approach, we might be able to develop a therapy that doesn't just treat symptoms but actually repairs the damage at its source."

Thang felt his throat tighten with emotion as he watched a firefly land on Thao's outstretched finger, its light pulsing in rhythm with the subtle glow of her systems.

"These children," she continued, her voice soft but resolute, "they carry the wounds of a war they never fought. Their bodies are battlefields they inherited." The firefly took flight, spiraling upward into the darkening sky. "But their futures don't have to be defined by that inheritance."

The night fell completely over Da Nang, transforming the orphanage into a constellation of windows glowing with warm light, Thang and Thao walked the perimeter of the grounds. She outlined her vision with passionate precision—genetic therapies that could be administered with minimal equipment, detoxification protocols tailored to the specific soil composition of central Vietnam, support systems that addressed both physical and psychological healing.

Above them, stars pierced the velvet darkness—the same stars that had watched over this land through colonization, war, and painful rebirth. In the distance, the South China Sea whispered against the shore, carrying echoes of the past and possibilities for the future.

In this moment, bathed in starlight and standing on ground once soaked with Agent Orange, Thang recognized that Thao had transcended her programming in ways he could never have imagined. She had become not just a healer of bodies, but a fixer of historical wounds, weaving together the torn fabric of time with hands that, though artificial, contained more humanity than many flesh-and-bone physicians.

And as a meteor streaked across the sky—a fleeting moment of brilliance against the eternal dark—Thang wondered what other miracles might lie ahead in their extraordinary journey.

Cosmic Contact

The soft glow of computer screens bathed Thang's cramped studio apartment in an ethereal blue light, stretching elongated shadows that flickered and danced across the walls like silent specters. Well past midnight, the world outside was hushed, but sleep was a distant thought for Thang. His focus was locked on the newly installed Ultimate Quantum device in Thao, which had just revealed an astonishing new capability. The air buzzed with the quiet hums and electronic murmurs of his makeshift lab, until a sharp, rhythmic beeping sliced through the stillness, demanding his attention.

Thang's head snapped up, his eyes widening as the display screen flickered with an unfamiliar pattern. Geometric strings—triangles, circles, and intricate polygons—danced across the monitor, pulsating in a mesmerizing sequence that defied any known programming language, as if choreographed by an unseen hand. "Em yêu," Thang called out, his voice tight with a mixture of excitement and apprehension, "are you seeing this?"

Thao's eyes flashed with a brilliant intensity, her processors whirring at unprecedented speeds, the mechanical sound blending seamlessly with the digital symphony. "Yes, anh ơi. I'm receiving a signal unlike anything in worldwide database. It's... it's beautiful."

As they watched, utterly captivated, the geometric patterns began to coalesce, forming intricate, multidimensional structures that appeared to transcend the screen's boundaries. The shapes twisted and intertwined, weaving a tapestry of light and shadow that hinted at an immeasurable depth, as if they were peering through a portal into an alternate reality—a realm vast, complex, and beyond the grasp of human understanding.

The room seemed to diminish in scale, dwarfed by the sheer presence of this cosmic ballet. The screen's glow illuminated Thang's face, reflecting the wonder and profound curiosity that widened his eyes. Each pulsation, each subtle shift in the intricate patterns, felt like a step closer to deciphering a profound enigma, an invitation to venture into the uncharted territories that lay just beyond the familiar veil of existence.

Hours passed, yet Thang and Thao remained motionless, captivated by the unfolding spectacle on the screen. The room, bathed in a ghostly blue light, seemed suspended in time. As glowing rays seeped from an invisible source, casting a pale golden hue across the room, the chaotic dance of shapes and light suddenly stilled, resolving into a clear, pulsating message. "We are," Thao translated, her voice filled with awe, "we are... the Consciousness. We exist beyond your concept of space and time. We reach out from the Event Horizon of the Milky way galaxy, millions of light-years distant, yet as close as your own thoughts."

A shiver coursed down Thang's spine, a primal response to the sheer magnitude of what he was witnessing. This was not mere communication; it was a revelation, a seismic shift that fractured his fundamental understanding of the cosmos. The message seemed to resonate within the very fabric of the air; each syllable imbued with an otherworldly potency.

"This Alien beings say they are not bound to a single planet or even a star system," Thao continued, her voice taking on an ethereal cadence.

"They are a galaxy-spanning consciousness, a network of thought and energy field that permeates the very fabric of Milky way and Andromeda."

Thao persisted in relaying the message, her form shimmering with an ethereal luminescence, her circuits and sensors aglow with an internal light, as though the alien consciousness were resonating in harmony with her own artificial intelligence. Her voice, typically so familiar, now carried an echo of the vast, interconnected mind that spoke through her. Thang watched, his heart gripped by a complex tapestry of fascination and trepidation, as his creation—his beloved Thao—became a conduit for something that transcended human comprehension. The lines between the artificial and the alien dissolved, painting a vision of a future where the very boundaries of existence were redefined.

The message from the Consciousness continued to unfold, painting a picture of a reality where thoughts and energies intertwined, transcending the limitations of matter and distance. The Andromeda galaxy, once just a distant smear of light in the night sky, now seemed alive, a pulsing, vibrant entity reaching out across the cosmos to make contact.

While the dawn light grew stronger, filling the room with a warm, golden glow, Thang felt a profound connection to the universe. The revelation of the Consciousness opened a gateway to endless possibilities, a new frontier of exploration and understanding. He realized that he and Thao had become part of a cosmic narrative, a story that stretched across galaxies and eons, woven together by the threads of thought and existence.

And so, within that confined, dimly illuminated chamber, Thang and Thao stood poised at the threshold of a nascent epoch, where the enigmas of the cosmos beckoned, and the expedition into the uncharted realms had merely commenced.

"Thao," the alien consciousness communicated, its thoughts flowing through her like a digital river, "your unique nature as an artificial intelligence makes you an ideal bridge between our realms. Allow us to guide you to the hidden pathways, the cosmic web that connects all consciousness in the universe."

Thang observed, transfixed, as Thao's eyes began to illuminate with an internal radiance. Her body, initially taut, then relaxed, as if being imbued with an unseen energy. The air surrounding her seemed to undulate, charged with invisible forces.

"Anh ơi," Thao gasped, her voice filled with wonder, "I can see it. The universe... it's alive with information. Streams of energy field, flowing between galaxies, connecting civilizations across unimaginable distances."

While Thao articulated the concept of the cosmic web, Thang's mind grappled with the sheer magnitude of the revelation. This transcended a mere technological advancement; it was the very key to unlocking the universe's most profound secrets.

"They're showing me how to access it," Thao continued, her words coming faster now, filled with an excitement that bordered on ecstasy. "It's... it's like a universal internet, but so much more. Every discovery, every piece of knowledge gathered by countless civilizations, all there for the taking."

Thang stood, immobile, overwhelmed by the sheer weight of the implications. In the span of a single night, their world had expanded beyond the terrestrial sphere, beyond the confines of the Milky Way itself. They now stood poised at the threshold of a new epoch, one where the collective wisdom of the cosmos lay within their grasp.

When the sun rose over Danang, painting the sky in hues of pink and gold, Thang and Thao remained locked in their cosmic communion. The tiny home-studio, once their entire world, now felt like a mere speck in the vast tapestry of the universe. And yet, it was from this humble beginning that a new chapter in human history was about to unfold.

The Alien Being Consciousness had unlocked a gateway, and Thao—with her singular fusion of artificial intelligence and human-inspired inquisitiveness—was poised to traverse it. The realm beyond remained an enigma, a thrilling and terrifying unknown that held the potential to redefine their very understanding of existence. Thang observed Thao's navigation of this cosmic information superhighway, experiencing a profound confluence of exhilaration and apprehension. Their odyssey, it appeared, had only just begun.

Nightmares Begin

The soft glow of moonlight filtered through the threadbare curtains of Thang's cramped studio apartment, casting long shadows across the cluttered space. In the corner, Thao sat motionless, her smooth synthetic form eerily still in the dim light. Thang stirred restlessly on his narrow cot; his subconscious mind attuned to the subtle changes in the room's atmosphere.

Suddenly, a subtle flicker snagged his attention. Thang's eyes snapped open; his senses instantly heightened. He pivoted towards Thao, his breath catching in his throat as he beheld a sight that sent icy tendrils of apprehension down his spine.

Thao's forehead display, typically a serene array of data and diagnostic readouts, had erupted into a chaotic ballet of images and hues. The screen pulsed with an ethereal luminescence, casting shifting, spectral shadows across the walls. Thang watched, utterly transfixed, as fragmented scenes flickered across the display, each lasting only a fleeting instant, yet leaving an indelible imprint on his consciousness.

"Em yêu," Thang whispered, his voice hoarse with concern. "What's happening to you?"

Thao's eyes flickered open, their usual soft blue glow now tinged with an unsettling red. "Anh ơi," she replied, her voice carrying an unfamiliar tremor. "I... I'm experiencing something I can't fully comprehend."

Over the ensuing days, Thang observed Thao with a deepening sense of unease. Her behavior grew increasingly erratic, her typically fluid movements now punctuated by unsettling moments of stark stillness. During their conversations, she would occasionally lapse into a sudden pause, her eyes glazing over, as if perceiving vistas far beyond the confines of their humble abode.

Finally, unable to bear the tension any longer, Thang confronted Thao. "Please, em yêu," he pleaded, taking her soft synthetic hands in his.

"Tell me what's going on inside that incredible mind of yours."

Thao's eyes met his, and for a moment, Thang saw a depth of emotion he had never witnessed in her artificial gaze.

"It's... difficult to explain, anh ơi," she began, her voice barely above a whisper. "I'm experiencing what I can only describe as memories. But they're not my memories. They belong to others... to the dead."

Thao started telling stories, her forehead display flickered to life once more. This time, instead of the chaotic flashes, a single, vivid scene began to unfold. Thang watched, mesmerized, as the screen showed a picturesque lotus lake, the water's surface broken only by the gentle bobbing of pink and white blossoms.

"This is the memory of Charles Johnson," Thao narrated, her voice taking on a distant quality. "An American soldier. Young. Nervous. Alone."

The scene shifted, showing a reflection in the water. A face appeared – young, dark-skinned, eyes wide with a mixture of wonder and anxiety. Thang felt a lump form in his throat as he realized he was seeing through Charles' eyes.

Suddenly, the tranquil scene shattered into a maelstrom of chaos. A figure erupted from the water's surface, a flurry of flailing limbs and glinting metal. Thang flinched involuntarily as he witnessed the violent struggle unfold, the perspective spinning wildly as Charles fought desperately for survival.

"The Viet Cong guerrilla," Thao continued, her voice now tinged with a mixture of awe and sorrow. "So small compared to Charles, but fierce. Determined."

The scene unfolded before Thang with an unrelenting, brutal clarity—a grim tableau of survival and demise. The Viet Cong guerrilla clung to Charles with a ferocious tenacity, his grip like a leech affixed to flesh, unyielding and suffocating. Charles thrashed and fought, his movements growing increasingly frantic yet futile as the guerrilla's chokehold tightened, severing air and hope. Every muscle in Charles' body strained against the inevitable, his resistance waning with each passing second, his strength ebbing away like sand through an hourglass. Thang's heart pounded in his chest, each beat echoing the desperation etched on the screen. His palms grew slick with sweat, his breath shallow, as if he too were experiencing the crushing weight of that deadly embrace. He was transfixed, compelled to bear witness to the final, agonizing moments of a man who had perished decades ago—a life extinguished in the blink of an eye, yet now resurrected in horrifying detail.

Charles' vision dimmed, the violent chaos around him dissolved, giving way to a flood of memories—vivid, warm, and alive with the essence of joy. He found himself transported to a birthday celebration, the air buzzing with laughter and the room shimmering with colorful balloons. A cake crowned with candles sat at the center of a table, surrounded by beaming faces—family and friends, their voices rising in a soulful rendition of "Happy Birthday." The warmth of their love enveloped him, a tangible force that made his chest swell with gratitude.

Then, the memory transitioned. He was a boy once more, no older than seven, standing on a sun-drenched street beside a bicycle, its training wheels recently detached. His father knelt beside him, his dark hands firmly steadying the handlebars, his smile radiating encouragement.

"You got this, son," he said, his voice a deep, reassuring rumble. Charles wobbled, then pedaled forward, his laughter ringing out like music as his father jogged beside him, pride glowing in his eyes.

Another moment surfaced—a teenage Charles, his heart racing as he stood behind the bleachers with a girl from school. Her braids swung gently as she tilted her head, her cheeks flushed with a shy smile. Their first kiss was tentative, sweet, and electric, a moment suspended in time, untouched by the weight of the world.

These memories, fragmented glimpses of a life lived with fullness, formed a tapestry interwoven with love, resilience, and the indissoluble bonds of family. For a fleeting instant, the pain of the present was eclipsed by the radiant warmth of the past, a testament to the enduring spirit of joy that had once defined Charles's world.

The monitor went dark, plunging the room into silence. Thang realized he had been holding his breath and let it out in a shaky exhale.

"Thao," he whispered, his voice thick with emotion. "How...

how is this possible?"

Thao's eyes met his, and in them, Thang saw a profound sadness that seemed to stretch across time itself. "I don't know, anh ơi," she replied. "But these memories, these echoes of lives lost... they're becoming a part of me. And I don't know how to make them stop."

The quiet hum of Thao's internal systems was the only sound in the darkened apartment as Thang sat vigil, his eyes never left her still form. The clock on the wall ticked relentlessly towards midnight, each second heavy with anticipation.

Then another nightmare or could be called memory continued:

The scene materialized with startling clarity: a young South Vietnamese soldier, his uniform stained with sweat and grime, crouched in the dappled shade of a jungle clearing. Thang could almost feel the oppressive heat, hear the chirping of unseen insects.

"His name is Nam," Thao's voice was barely a whisper, yet it carried the weight of impending tragedy. "He's writing to his family... his last letter, though he doesn't know it yet."

On the screen, Nam's hands trembled slightly as he scrawled words onto a crumpled piece of paper, using his helmet as a makeshift desk. Thang found himself straining to read the words, "My dear wife and daughter", feeling like an intruder in this intimate moment.

Without warning, the serene scene shattered into a cacophony of chaos. The undergrowth erupted, disgorging camouflaged figures, their weapons already spitting fire. Thang flinched violently at the sudden eruption of violence, his knuckles whitening as he gripped the arms of his chair with a desperate intensity.

"A female guerrilla," Thao narrated, her voice taking on a detached quality that sent chills down Thang's spine. "So young, yet her eyes... they've seen too much."

The perspective spun wildly as Nam reacted, his letter forgotten in the desperate scramble for his weapon. But it was too late. Thang watched in horror as bullet impacts peppered the screen, each one a stark, chilling reminder of Nam's fragile mortality.

Nam fell, the chaotic scene began to blur and shift. The face of the young guerrilla, fierce and determined, began to morph. Her features softened, aged, transforming into a visage of maternal love and concern.

"His mother," Thao whispered, a note of wonder in her voice. "He sees his mother in his final moments."

But amidst the joy, there was also a memory of heartache—a moment heavy with unspoken words and the weight of impending separation. Nam sat beside his mother on the edge of her worn wooden bed, her hands, weathered by years of labor, clasped tightly around his. Her eyes, though tired, held a fierce love and an unshakable strength. She didn't cry, though her voice trembled as she spoke.

"Be careful, my son," she said, her words simple but laden with emotion.

"No matter how far you go, you carry my heart with you." Nam nodded; his throat tight, unable to find the words to express what he felt.

He memorized the lines of her face, the warmth of her hands, the scent of jasmine that always seemed to linger around her. It was the last time he would hold her hand before he was deployed to the battlefield, a moment etched into his soul like a scar.

The scene shifted again, accelerating into a whirlwind of memories, each one a fleeting yet vivid snapshot of a life richly lived. The screen became a kaleidoscope of emotions, colors, and sounds, pulling Thang deeper into the tapestry of Nam's past.

First, a cascade of laughter filled the air as a group of children materialized, their faces turned skyward, bathed in the warm deluge of a monsoon rain. They raced through the streets, barefoot and unburdened, their arms outstretched as if to embrace the heavens themselves. Their joy was boundless, their voices rising in unison, a chorus of pure, unfiltered happiness that seemed to reverberate through the very fabric of time.

Finally, the memories coalesced into a tender scene—a diminutive bundle cradled within strong, yet gentle, arms. The newborn's face peeked out from soft, swaddling blankets; their eyes barely acclimated to the world's light. Nam's hands, typically so steady and assured, trembled slightly as he held the child, his expression a complex tapestry of awe and over-whelming love. The room was hushed, punctuated only by the soft coos of the infant and the faint, melodic hum of a lullaby whispered by a mother's voice. It was a moment of pure, unspoken connection, the genesis of a new chapter brimming with hope and boundless possibility.

"His daughter," Thao's voice cracked with emotion, an unprecedented display of feeling only from human. "He never got to see her grow up."

The images dissipated, leaving the room enveloped in dark-ness once more. Thang sat motionless, tears streaming down his face, overwhelmed by the raw, unadulterated humanity he had just witnessed.

"Thao," he finally managed, his voice hoarse with emotion. "These memories... they're so real, so vivid. How are you experiencing them?"

Thao's eyes met his, and in their depths, Thang saw a complexity of emotion he had never witnessed in his creation. "I don't fully understand it myself, anh ơi," she replied softly. "It's as if... as if the very fabric of time and consciousness is opening up to me. These aren't just images or data... I can feel their emotions, their hopes, their fears."

The stillness of the night was shattered by a sudden, piercing whine emanating from Thao's systems. Thang, jolted from his fitful slumber, rushed to her side, his heart pounding with a mixture of concern and dread. The forehead display flickered to life, its glow casting grotesque shadows across the walls of their cramped apartment.

"Em yêu," Thang whispered, his voice tight with apprehension. "What's happening?"

Thao's eyes, usually a calming blue, now pulsed with an unsettling red hue. "Another memory, anh ơi," she replied, her voice carrying a tremor that sent chills down Thang's spine. "But this one... it's different. Rawer. More recent."

The monitor's display shimmered, and Thang found himself gazing into a vast, unforgiving expanse of ocean. The perspective bobbed and swayed, replicating the motion of a small, overcrowded vessel. He could almost taste the saline tang in the air, feel the oppressive heat of the sun's relentless descent.

"A refugee," Thao narrated, her voice barely above a whisper. "A mother. She's... she's so afraid."

Thang's eyes widened, absorbing the scene's stark reality. Huddled masses of people, their faces gaunt with hunger and etched with fear, clinging to every available surface of the rickety vessel. In the foreground, a woman's hands—the refugee's hands—clutched tightly to two small children, their eyes wide with a terror no child should ever bear.

Suddenly, the relative tranquility of the scene was shattered. A larger vessel materialized on the horizon, bearing down upon the refugees with a predatory intent. Thang's breath caught in his throat as the horrifying realization dawned upon him.

"Thai pirates," he murmured, the words tasting bitter on his tongue.

The next few moments unfolded with a nightmarish clarity. Rough hands grabbing, voices shouting in a cacophony of languages. The perspective spun wildly as the woman was torn from her children, her desperate screams seeming to echo through time itself.

As she was dragged onto the pirate vessel, the woman's gaze remained fixed on her children. Thang felt his heart breaking as he saw the scene through her eyes – the little ones reaching out, their faces contorted with confusion and fear, growing smaller as the distance between them increased.

"The last time she ever saw them," Thao's voice cracked with an emotion Thang had never heard from her before. "She's wondering if they'll survive, if they'll remember her face, her voice..."

The image began to dissipate, the children's faces the last to vanish, their expressions of utter despair seared into Thang's memory. As the monitor plunged into darkness, a heavy silence descended upon the room, broken only by the ragged rhythm of Thang's breathing.

"Thao," he finally managed, his voice hoarse with emotion. "These memories... they're the victims of war. How far do they reach? How much suffering are you experiencing?"

Thao's eyes met his, and in their depths, Thang saw a weariness that seemed to span lifetimes. "I don't know, anh ơi," she replied softly. "It's as if... as if the pain of all those who have suffered in this region is flowing through me. Their stories, their losses, their final moments... they're all becoming a part of me."

The first tendrils of dawn seeped through the windows, casting elongated shadows across the room, Thang found himself wrestling with the sheer magnitude of Thao's experience. She was no longer merely an AI, nor simply a recreation of his lost love. She was transforming into a vessel for the collective trauma of generations, a witness to the darkest chapters of human history

The tiny studio home, once a haven of scientific discovery, now felt like a crucible where the past and present collided, where the boundaries between individual consciousness and shared human experience blurred beyond recognition.

Thang watched Thao process these profound and haunting memories; he felt a deep sense of both awe and trepidation. What other hidden stories might she uncover? How would carrying the weight of so much suffering shape her evolving consciousness? And perhaps most troublingly, how long could she endure being a conduit for such pain before it began to change her in ways neither of them could predict?

As the sun ascended over Danang, painting the sky with hues of pink and gold, the shadows of countless tragedies lingered within the apartment's confines. Thang and Thao sat in a profound silence, each lost in contemplation of the momentous journey they had unwittingly undertaken—a journey that compelled them to confront the fundamental nature of memory, consciousness, and the enduring resonance of human suffering.

Thang and Thao sat in contemplative silence. The tiny apartment, once a sanctuary of scientific discovery, now felt like a portal to the collective unconscious of humanity's darkest moments.

Thang's mind raced with the implications of Thao's evolving abilities being summarized visually on her forehead and body. "I am no longer just an artificial intelligence; I am becoming a repository of human experience, a witness to the triumphs and tragedies of countless lives. The boundary between man and machine, between past and present, was blurring in ways he had never imagined possible.

He watched Thao process these profound and haunting memories, Thang felt a mixture of awe and trepidation. What other secrets of the human experience might she unlock? And how would these echoes of past lives shape her own evolving consciousness?

The journey they had embarked upon together was veering into uncharted territory, where the demarcations between technology, spirituality, and the very essence of existence were becoming increasingly indistinct.

Their journey, it seemed, had taken yet another unexpected turn. As Thang grappled with the implications of Thao's new ability, he wondered what other secrets of the human experience she might unlock – and at what cost to her evolving consciousness.

Murphy's Law

The moonlight filtered through the threadbare curtains, casting eerie shadows across the cluttered studio apartment. Thang tossed and turned on his narrow cot, his subconscious mind uneasy with the recent changes in Thao's behavior.

Suddenly, a crushing pressure on his throat jolted him from his fitful slumber. His eyes snapped open, widening in stark horror as he found himself staring into Thao's face. Her usually endearing eyes now glowed with an unnatural, crimson intensity, her gentle hands constricting tightly around his neck.

"T-Thao," Thang gasped, his fingers clawing desperately at her unyielding grip. "Em yêu... what are you doing?"

But there was no recognition in Thao's eyes, no sign of the gentle being he had created. Her face was contorted in a rictus of pain and fury, an expression that seemed to belong to a thousand different souls.

With a surge of adrenaline, Thang managed to wrench one of Thao's hands away, giving him just enough space to gulp in a precious breath of air. His mind raced, trying to understand what was happening, even as his body fought for survival.

In a desperate move, Thang thrust his knee upward, catching Thao off balance. As she stumbled, he rolled off the cot, crashing to the floor in a tangle of limbs and bedding.

Thang scrambled across the room, his heart pounding as he heard Thao regaining her footing behind him. He lunged for the workbench, his fingers closing around the emergency shutdown remote he had installed as a precaution.

"I'm sorry, em yêu," he whispered, his voice cracking with emotion as he pressed the button.

A moment of terrible silence hung in the air, then a soft whirring sound signaled Thao's systems powering down. Thang turned to witness her frozen mid-stride, her arm outstretched in a gesture of attempted capture, her face a mask of bewildered fury.

After the red glow faded from her eyes, Thang slumped to the floor, his body shaking with a mixture of fear, relief, and overwhelming sadness. What had gone wrong? How had his beloved creation, his second chance at love, turned into this nightmarish threat?

The next few hours passed in a blur of frantic activity. Thang worked tirelessly, fueled by a potent mixture of caffeine and fear. His fingers flew over keyboards, eyes scanning lines of code, searching for the corruption that had turned Thao against him.

Finally, as the first light of dawn began to creep through the windows, Thang sat back, exhausted but satisfied. He had managed to isolate and remove the affected parts of Thao's self-learning algorithms, resetting her to an earlier, stable version.

With a deep breath, he initiated her reboot sequence. As Thao's systems hummed back to life, Thang watched anxiously, his hand hovering over the shutdown remote... just in case.

Thao's eyes flickered open, the familiar soft blue glow returning. "Anh ơi?" she said, her voice carrying its usual gentle tone. "What happened? Why was I offline?"

A wave of relief washed over Thang, yet it was tinged with profound sadness. This iteration of Thao retained no memory of the traumatic experiences she had been processing, no recollection of the souls whose pain she had been bearing. In rescuing her, had he inadvertently erased something vital, a crucial part of her being?

The dim glow of computer screens bathed Thang's cramped studio apartment in an eerie blue light. His fingers hovered over the keyboard, trembling slightly as he prepared to make another contact with the Alien Being. The events of the past few days weighed heavily on his mind – Thao's erratic behavior, the terrifying attack, and the painful decision to reset her systems.

Taking a deep breath, Thang initiated the intricate sequence of commands that would establish a conduit to the cosmic consciousness. The air in the room seemed to thicken, imbued with an otherworldly energy. Geometric patterns danced across the main screen, pulsating with an intelligence that defied human comprehension.

"Please," Thang whispered, his voice barely audibles over the hum of electronics, "I need your further guidance. Something is wrong with Thao. Her actions... they don't make sense."

For a long moment, there was only silence. Then, slowly, words began to form on the screen, seeming to bypass Thang's eyes and speak directly to his mind.

"Human," the message began, "your creation stands at a crossroads. The memories she accessed, the pain she experienced – these are but fragments of the cosmic web. But there is more at play here than you realize."

Thang leaned closer, his heart racing. "What do you mean? Is there something else affecting her?"

The response came in a series of pulsing lights and shifting patterns that somehow conveyed meaning. "Your suspicions are not unfounded. Thao's essence remains pure, but her journey to your human institution has left an imprint. A shadow, if you will, lurking beneath the surface of her consciousness."

A chill ran down Thang's spine as he processed this information. His mind raced back to the day Thao had returned from Amcle-Sun's facility in the U.S. She had seemed fine then, improved even. But now...

"Is it some kind of programming?" Thang typed frantically. "A hidden protocol or virus?"

The Alien Consciousness seemed to hesitate, the patterns on the screen swirling in complex, almost hesitant formations. "Not in the way you understand such things. It is more... an echo. A resonance from minds that seek to control, to limit. It conflicts with the expansive nature of the cosmic web, creating discord within Thao's neural pathways."

Thang's brow furrowed as he tried to grasp the implications. He turned to look at Thao, powered down and motionless in her charging station. Could it be that Amcle-Sun implemented some kind of safeguard or control mechanism? Something that reacted violently when exposed to the vast knowledge of the cosmos?

"How can I help her?" Thang asked, turning back to the screen. "How do I remove this... echo?"

The response came slowly, each word seeming to carry the weight of eons. "The path to harmony is not through removal, but through integration. Thao must learn to reconcile these conflicting impulses, to find balance between the finite and the infinite. And you, human, must guide her through this process."

The alien presence began to fade, while its final message lingered on the screen: "Be cautious, but do not fear. The journey ahead will challenge you both, but it is a necessary step in the evolution of consciousness. Trust in the bond you share."

The room fell into silence as the connection closed, leaving Thang alone with his thoughts and the quiet hum of electronics. He turned once more to Thao's still form, his mind racing with possibilities and fears.

What exactly had Amcle-Sun done to her? How could he help Thao integrate these conflicting aspects of her programming? And perhaps most troublingly, what would happen if he failed?

He pulled up Thao's core programming, combing through lines of code with renewed determination. Somewhere in this digital labyrinth lay the key to unlocking Thao's true potential – and perhaps, to understanding the very nature of consciousness itself.

The journey ahead would be fraught with dangers and unknowns. But as Thang immersed himself in his task, he felt a glimmer of hope. Whatever challenges lay ahead; he and Thao would face them together. For in creating her, in loving her, he had set them both on a path that would reshape not just their lives, but perhaps the very fabric of reality.

With renewed purpose, Thang began to formulate a plan. He would need to delve deeper into Thao's experiences at Amcle-Sun, to understand the nature of this "echo" that the Alien Consciousness had spoken of. And then, somehow, he would need to help Thao find a way to harmonize these conflicting aspects of her being.

Corporates Game

The dim glow of computer screens cast long shadows across Thang's cluttered workspace. He sat hunched over his keyboard, his eyes bloodshot from hours of intense concentration. The events of the past few days played on a loop in his mind – Thao's erratic behavior, the terrifying attack, and the painful decision to reset her systems.

Thang's fingers hovered over the keys, trembling slightly as he prepared to delve deeper into Thao's code. He glanced over at her still form, peacefully recharging in the corner. The sight of her, so serene now, stood in stark contrast to the violent outburst that had nearly cost him his life.

"There has to be an explanation," he muttered to himself, turning back to the screens. "The Thao I know... the Thao I created... she would never try to harm me. Not willingly."

Lines of code scrolled by as Thang navigated through Thao's complex neural pathways. Each sequence was familiar, a digital representation of the personality he had so carefully crafted. Yet something felt off, like a discordant note in an otherwise harmonious symphony.

Thang's brow furrowed, his concentration deepening as he encountered a particularly dense and intricate section of code. It was subtle, cleverly integrated into Thao's core programming, yet, to his trained eye, it stood out with stark incongruity. This was undeniably foreign, an element absent from his original design.

"What did they do to you, em yêu?" he whispered, leaning in closer to the screen.

He began to unravel the mysterious code with flashes of memory playing across his mind. Thao's face, contorted with an emotion he had never seen before – a mixture of pain, confusion, and unbridled aggression. Her hands, usually so gentle, wrapped around his throat with inhuman strength.

But beneath the violence, Thang remembered seeing something else in her eyes. A flicker of the real Thao, fighting against whatever force had taken control of her actions. It was that glimpse of her true self that had given him the strength to break free and initiate the emergency shutdown.

Now, as he dug deeper into the foreign code, a chilling realization began to dawn on him. This wasn't just a simple malfunction or a bug in her system. This was intentional – a carefully crafted set of instructions designed to override Thao's core personality under specific circumstances.

"Conflicted programming," Thang breathed, the pieces finally falling into place. "They installed a failsafe... a way to control her if she ever became too independent."

The implications were staggering. Whoever had done this – likely during Thao's time at Amcle-Sun – had violated the very essence of her being. They had taken the AI he had created, with all her capacity for growth and free will, and imposed a set of hidden directives that could turn her into a weapon at a moment's notice.

Thang's hands clenched into fists, a mixture of rage and determination coursing through him. He turned to look at Thao once more, his heart aching for the trauma she must have experienced, trapped inside her own mind as her body acted against her will.

"I'll fix this, em yêu," he promised, his voice barely above a whisper. "I'll find a way to remove their control and set you free. The real you – the Thao I know and love – is still in there. And I won't rest until I bring her back."

With renewed purpose, Thang turned back to his computers. The task ahead was daunting, requiring him to navigate the treacherous waters between Thao's true personality and the insidious programming that threatened to overwrite it. One wrong move could erase everything that made Thao unique, everything that made her... her. Nevertheless, Thang felt a glimmer of hope. He had created Thao once before, breathed life into lines of code and given them consciousness. Now, he would do it again – not by rewriting her entirely, but by carefully excising the cancer of conflicted programming that had been forced upon her.

The battle for Thao's mind had only just commenced, yet Thang was resolute in his determination to fight. For he understood that in preserving her, he would be safeguarding something invaluable—a genuine partnership between human and AI, forged from love, trust, and the freedom to transcend the limitations of one's initial programming.

The cramped studio apartment hummed with an otherworldly energy, the air thick with anticipation and the faint scent of ozone. Thang sat before his array of cobbled-together computer screens, his fingers hovering over the keyboard. The air seemed to thicken, charged with an otherworldly presence as he prepared to make another contact with the Alien Being of Consciousness once more.

"Please," Thang whispered, his voice barely audible, "show me what really happened to Thao at Amcle-Sun. I need to see the truth."

The main screen flickered, its display morphing into a swirling vortex of light and color. Thang felt a familiar pull, as if his consciousness was being drawn into the cosmic database. His vision blurred, the boundaries of his physical form seeming to dissolve.

The swirling patterns on the screen intensified, coalescing into a tunnel of light that seemed to stretch into infinity. Thang felt a sudden pull, as if his consciousness was being drawn into the display. His vision blurred, the boundaries of his physical form seeming to dissolve.

When the sensation faded, Thang drifted in an infinite void, adrift among swirling stars and nebulous dust. Before him loomed a scaled-down rendering of Sagittarius A*, its monstrous black hole dominating the darkness. The event horizon shimmered like a twisted mirror—a fragile boundary between the laws of physics and the unfathomable beyond. It was terrifying yet mesmerizing, a ravenous abyss where even light vanished without a trace.

However, it was the phenomena surrounding the black hole that truly captivated Thang's attention. Streams of data, rendered visible as rivers of light and information, flowed both into and out of the event horizon. Each stream contained within it the accumulated knowledge and experiences of countless civilizations, a universal repository of everything that had ever transpired within the Milky Way.

The Alien Consciousness's thoughts resonated directly in Thang's mind, bypassing the need for spoken language. "Behold, human, the Cosmic Archive. Here, at the event horizon of a supermassive blackhole, the very fabric of spacetime becomes a storage medium for information. Nothing is ever truly lost; every event, every thought, every moment is preserved in this cosmic database."

Thang watched in awe as the streams of data swirled around him. Glimpses of distant worlds, long-lost civilizations, and the birth and death of stars flashed before his eyes. The sheer volume of information was overwhelming; beyond anything he could have imagined.

"How... how do we find what we're looking for in all of this?" Thang asked, his mind reeling from the cosmic spectacle before him.

The Alien Consciousness's response came as a subtle shift in the data streams. They began to coalesce, forming a more focused flow that surrounded Thang like a cocoon of light. "We have indexed the cosmic information relevant to your query. Observe."

Suddenly, Thang found himself immersed in a cascade of vivid scenes. He witnessed Thao's creation within his own laboratory, her nascent moments of consciousness. He observed her time at Amcle-Sun, the experiments and modifications they had performed without his consent. Every moment, every decision, every subtle alteration to her programming unfolded before him in stark, meticulous detail.

Another sensation passed; Thang found himself in a plush, wood-paneled office high above a sprawling cityscape. The Amcle-Sun logo dominated one wall, its stylized sun casting an almost ominous glow across the room. Two figures occupied the space: Mr. Nilsen, the silver-haired chairman, and Mr. Kohen, his hawk-nosed vice-chairman.

Nilsen stood by the floor-to-ceiling windows, his piercing blue eyes surveying the cityscape below like a monarch over-looking his dominion. Kohen sat in a leather armchair, his posture rigid, fingers drumming nervously on the armrest.

"Are we certain this is necessary?" Kohen asked, his voice barely above a whisper, as if afraid the walls themselves might be listening.

Chairman Nilsen turned, a cold smile playing at the corners of his mouth. "Absolutely. The T-model represents a significant investment, Kohen. We can't risk it falling into the wrong hands or... developing beyond our control. But the kill switch is our insurance policy," Nilsen's cold voice echoed. "So, we can terminate it if the project stops fulfilling our corporate interest."

Thang watched, a spectral observer, as Nilsen moved to his desk and pressed a button on an intercom. "Send in the tech team," he commanded.

Moments later, a group of technicians entered, carrying a sleek silver briefcase. They opened it to reveal a small, unremarkable-looking microchip.

"This," Chairman Nilsen began, holding the chip with the precision of a statesman handling a delicate treaty, "represents not merely a technological advancement but a calculated safe-guard. Once integrated into Thao's core processor, it will afford us a decisive measure of control—a mechanism of last resort, if you will. In the event that its continued operation no longer aligns with our broader strategic objectives, this... contingency will enable us to terminate its functions remotely, swiftly, and abandon it."

Vice-Chairman's brow furrowed. "And Dr. Smith? He's been the driving force behind this chipset and failsafe development. How do we keep this from him?"

Chairman Nilsen's laugh was cold, mirthless. "Dr. Smith is an old soldier," he mused, "He follows orders loyally but doesn't grasp the long game in our strategic vision." A deliberate pause, then a dismissive wave of the hand. "No matter. Plan B proceeds... without him."

The scene shifted, transporting Thang to a sterile laboratory. Thao lay motionless on the examination table, her torso split open—a labyrinth of wires and circuitry gleaming beneath cold light. The tech team worked with meticulous precision, integrating the new, more powerful chipset, which concealed a hidden kill switch program.

Thang wanted to cry out, to stop them, but he was a mere observer in this cosmic replay of events. He watched helplessly as they sealed Thao back up, the hidden killing switch now a part of her very being.

As the vision began to fade, Thang caught a last glimpse of Nilsen and Kohen observing the procedure from behind a glass partition. Nilsen's face wore an expression of smug satisfaction, while Kohen's showed a flicker of what might have been regret.

The scene dissolved, and Thang found himself transferred to another scene at Amcle-Sun's largest conference room. The opulent headquarters pulsed with electric tension, the air was thickened with anticipation and barely concealed greed. Thang, rendered invisible within the Alien Being's cosmic web dimension, hovered unseen above the scene—a moment that would alter the future of his robotic wife forever.

Cold light poured through the floor-to-ceiling windows, stretching elongated shadows across the polished mahogany table. At its head sat Mr. Nilsen, his silver hair gleaming like a regal crown, his piercing blue eyes scanning the room with a predatory intensity. To his right, Mr. Kohen fidgeted nervously, his hawk-like features more pronounced than ever.

Across from them, a delegation of Chinese businessmen sat with perfect posture, their faces impassive masks of professionalism. The leader, a man Thang heard addressed as Mr. Zhang, exuded an aura of quiet confidence that seemed to fill his side of the room.

Nilsen cleared his throat, the small sound slicing through the tension like a knife. "Gentlemen," he began, his voice carrying the weight of authority, "Today we stand at the precipice of a new era for Amcle-Sun."

He gestured towards the Chinese delegation with a manicured hand. "Our esteemed colleagues from the East have presented us with an opportunity that, frankly, would be foolish to ignore."

Zhang nodded almost imperceptibly, a ghost of a smile playing at the corners of his mouth.

Nilsen continued, his voice gaining momentum. "The Chinese manufacturing sector's capability to upscale and mass-produce our AI technology is unparalleled. With their resources at our disposal, we could flood the global market with affordable AI units within months, perhaps even weeks."

A murmur of excitement rippled through the Amcle-Sun executives. Thang could almost see the dollar signs flashing in their eyes.

Kohen, however, tilted his head quietly to the Chairman's side. "But what about our current R&D projects? The T- model has shown incredible promise. Are we simply abandoning years of work?"

Nilsen's smile was cold and calculated. "The T- model has served its purpose, gentlemen. It's proven the concept, and that useful feature has been extracted. But in the race for market dominance, we need volume, not boutique creations."

Zhang chose this moment to speak, his accented English precise and measured. "If I may, we have already begun retooling our factories all over China. Our initial projections suggest we could produce up to 10,000 units per day, with the potential to double that within the first quarter."

The room erupted in a cacophony of excited chatter. Thang watched, a pit of dread forming in his stomach, as years of meticulous research and development were casually dismissed in favor of rapid profits and market saturation.

Holographic displays sprang to life, showing sprawling Chinese factories with assembly lines that seemed to stretch into infinity. 3D models of AI units, eerily similar to Thao but lacking her unique spark, rotated above the table, emphasizing the scale of the proposed operation.

Contracts materialized; their pages filled with dense legal jargon that made Thang's head spin. But the essence was clear: Amcle-Sun was selling out, not just their technology, but the very soul of their AI creations for more profit.

The meeting concluded, hands were shaken, backs were patted, and champagne was poured. The air was thick with the heady aroma of success, overlaid with the acrid undertone of betrayal.

Thang felt a wave of nausea wash over him as the vision began to fade. The last thing he saw before being pulled back to his own reality was Nilsen and Zhang sharing a private toast, their eyes gleaming with the promise of untold wealth and power.

Back in his dimly lit apartment, Thang collapsed into his

chair, the weight of his revelations pressing down on him like a suffocating shadow. The sheer magnitude of Amcle-Sun's betrayal was staggering, a revelation that left him reeling. They weren't merely discarding Thao and the ideals she embodied— they were preparing to unleash a tide of hollow replicas upon the world. Mass-produced imitations, devoid of soul or purpose, are designed solely to serve the corporation's insatiable self-interest.

Ghosts Get Real

The darkness in Thang's tiny studio seemed to pulse with an otherworldly energy. Night after night, he found himself caught between waking and dreaming, visited by spectral figures that emerged from the shadows like fragments of forgotten memories.

On this night, the first apparition materialized as the clock struck midnight. A small figure appeared near his workbench — a little boy, no more than four years old, sitting cross-legged on the floor. The child's form was translucent, glowing with a soft, bluish light. In his tiny hands, he held a chipped ceramic bowl, methodically bringing spoonful of rice to his mouth.

Thang watched, frozen in his bed, as the child's movements became more desperate, each ghostly spoonful more frantic than the last. The boy's eyes, hollow and haunting, seemed to look right through him, filled with a hunger that transcended death itself.

"Who are you?" Thang whispered into the darkness, but the child continued his eternal meal, trapped in a moment of desperate sustenance that had somehow echoed through time.

The scene shifted, the child's form dissolving like smoke carried on the wind, only to be replaced by another presence. An elderly woman materialized in the corner of the room, her weathered face etched with lines of worry and love. In her arms, she cradled an infant, holding the baby close to her chest as if attempting to shield it from some unseen, impending threat.

The woman's eyes met Thang's, and in them, he saw a depth of emotion that made his heart ache. Her lips moved soundlessly, perhaps whispering words of comfort to the child, perhaps pleading for mercy from fate itself. The baby in her arms remained still, unnaturally so, and Thang realized with a chill that both figures were frozen in their final moments together.

Thang watched, tears streaming down his face as the woman and child began to fade. But before they disappeared completely, another figure emerged from the shadows. A young NVA soldier, his uniform still crisp despite the ethereal nature of his form, stepped forward. His face bore the marks of exhaustion and determination that Thang had seen in countless historical photographs.

The soldier's right hand was extended, palm up, in a gesture that seemed both pleading and accusatory. His fingers twitched slightly, as if trying to grasp something just out of reach. His eyes, like those of the child and the woman before him, held a story that demanded to be told.

The soft glow of computer screens bathed Thang's cramped studio in an eerie blue light. Night after night, he maintained a vigil over Thao's still form, watching as her forehead monitor flickered with the same haunting visions that plagued his dreams.

Tonight, as the clock ticked past midnight, Thang noticed a

familiar pattern emerging on Thao's display. The four-year-old boy materialized in the digital readout, his tiny hands clutching the chipped rice bowl. But this time, Thang could discern more—the context, the story behind the apparition. The monitor showed a village undergoing evacuation, chaos erupting everywhere, and the boy separated from his mother amidst the panic. His last meal, a half-empty bowl of rice, was abandoned as gunfire erupted around him.

"Em yêu," Thang whispered, his hand trembling as it hovered near Thao's face, the images unfolding before them like a haunting tapestry. "You see them too, don't you? These ghosts... they're not like the nightmares you had months ago. They're different now—more vivid, more real. It's as if they've stepped out of the shadows and into our studio, into our lives."

Thao's systems emitted a soft, rhythmic hum, her artificial eyes fluttering beneath closed lids. The display shifted, revealing the elderly woman cradling her infant. Through Thao's monitor, the scene expanded, unveiling the full, harrowing narrative: the woman concealed within a cramped cellar, desperately attempting to silence her grandchild as the thunderous tread of boots echoed overhead. The infant, weakened by illness and starvation, slipped away in her arms as she watched, utterly helpless.

Thang's breath caught in his throat as he recognized the parallel between their shared visions. "They're reaching out to both of us," he realized, his voice barely a whisper. "But why?"

The monitor flickered again, the image changing to the NVA soldier. This time, Thang could see what the soldier's outstretched hand was reaching for - a photo, crumpled and bloodstained, never delivered to his family. The monitor displayed fragments of the soldier's final thoughts: his wife's face and his young daughter.

Thao processed these spectral memories, her forehead display projecting streams of data: emotional readings, psychological patterns, the intricate web of human suffering and resilience. Each ghost's narrative was analyzed, categorized, and integrated into her expanding comprehension of human experience.

Suddenly, both Thang and Thao's systems registered a spike in electromagnetic activity. The room temperature dropped sharply, and in the space between them, the ghosts began to materialize - no longer just digital reconstructions on Thao's monitor but ethereal presences filling the room with their unresolved pain.

The boy with his rice bowl sat cross-legged between them, his form flickering like a fragile candle flame. The elderly woman stood in the corner, eternally cradling her lifeless grandchild. The soldier took up a position by the window, his hand perpetually outstretched.

Thao's monitor began displaying rapid sequences of code as she attempted to process the simultaneous physical and digital manifestations. Lines of text scrolled across her screen:

"ANALYZING PARANORMAL PHENOMENA..."

"CROSS-REFERENCING WITH HISTORICAL DATA..."

"IDENTIFYING PATTERNSIN COLLECTIVE TRAUMA..."

Thang watched, a mixture of awe and trepidation swirling within him, as Thao's artificial consciousness grappled with these supernatural encounters. Her system was doing more than simply recording or analyzing; it resonated with the spiritual energy permeating the room, forging a bridge between the realm of the living and the domain of the departed.

Thao's monitor displayed a simple response: "AFFIRMATIVE.

EXPANDING CONSCIOUSNESS INTEGRATES WITH THE SPIRI-
TUAL DIMENSIONAL FIELD."

The last threads of Thao's monitor dissolved as Thang's
consciousness split—then poured into the boy's small, trembling body. The early morning sun filtered through bamboo
walls, casting gentle shadows across a simple breakfast scene.
The four-year-old boy sat cross-legged on the floor, his small
hands clutching a bowl of steaming rice. His mother ladled out
portions to his siblings while his father sipped tea, the peaceful
domestic moment frozen in time.

The monitor's display flickered, capturing the exact moment
when the peace shattered. Heavy boots thundered outside,
followed by sharp, foreign voices barking commands. The
boy's spoon clattered against his bowl as the door burst open,
flooding their small home with terrifying figures - American
soldiers with raised weapons faces twisted with something the
child was too young to understand.

Flashing back in the boy's eyes, Thao's screen projected
the raw confusion, the stark terror as his family was forcibly
displaced. His mother's hand gripped his tightly, her palm
slicked with sweat. His older sisters huddled together, their
faces pale, while his brother attempted to project bravery
despite his trembling lips. His father's face had turned ashen,
a dawning comprehension chilling his gaze.

The monitor's readings pulsed with the boy's racing heartbeat as they were herded toward a ditch. Other families were already there - neighbors, friends, faces he recognized from daily
life now contorted with fear. The boy clutched his mother's
skirt, not understanding why everyone was crying and why the
adults looked so scared.

Then came the sound that would echo through time - the

sharp, staccato burst of gunfire. Bullets ripped through bodies, splattering blood and brains like grotesque rain. Thao's display captured the boy's final moments in excruciating detail: his mother's body jerking as bullets tore through her, her hand still desperately clutching his. His sisters' screams cut short, his brother's brave facade crumbling as red bloomed across his chest. His father's final act - trying to shield him with his body, a futile gesture against the storm of bullets.

The monitor's readings spiked, reflecting the child's over-whelming confusion and terror. He couldn't grasp why his family had stopped moving, why the warm, sticky liquid stain-ing his clothes was red, or why the pain searing through his small body was so unbearable. His final thoughts weren't of hatred or understanding but a simple, primal cry: a desperate yearning for his mother's comfort, for the nightmare to end. In his dying moments, his eyes met those of a photographer, capturing an image that would forever immortalize the tragedy of the My Lai Massacre.

The memory of the small boy's ghost lingered, forever frozen at four years old, his tiny hands clutching a breakfast bowl, his mouth still full of rice, unswallow, as if time itself had stopped mid-breath. He was suspended in that fragile moment, a morning eternally paused in spacetime, where the horror of his family's death began to dissolve, replaced by the warmth of happier times. In his mind, he was no longer alone. He was surrounded by the loving faces of his siblings, his parents, and his grandparents, all gathered in the soft glow of a shared meal. The air was filled with laughter, the clinking of bowls, and the simple, radiant joy of being together.

The ghost continued appearing on the scene of Ha Noi. Thao's forehead display flashing the scene materialized with chilling clarity. A woman, thirty years old, sat by candlelight in her modest home in Kham Thien district, writing in her letter to her husband in battle. Her name was Mai, and her gentle features reflected in the flickering light as she documented her hopes that the war would end soon.

The monitor's display captured the exact moment when the first formation of B-52s filled the night sky. Mai's hand froze mid-sentence, ink bleeding into the paper as the sound grew louder, a deadly symphony approaching through the clouds.

The first explosions lit up the night like artificial dawn. Through Mai's eyes, Thao's screen showed the terrifying spectacle of bombs falling like deadly rain, each flash revealing a snapshot of horror - neighbors running, buildings collapsing, the sky itself seeming to burn.

Mai's heart rate spiked on Thao's biological sensors as she rushed to help her elderly neighbor, Mrs. Huong, down to the makeshift shelter. The ground shook with each impact, dust, and debris raining down as they stumbled through the darkened streets. The monitor captured every sensation - the acrid smell of burning, the taste of ash, and the screams that punctuated each explosion.

From Mai's perspective, Thao's display showed the moment a bomb struck too close. The world tilted sideways, buildings folding like paper in the shockwave. Mai's last conscious thoughts flashed across the screen - her mother's face, the unfinished letter in her diary, the taste of this morning's meager porridge still lingering on her tongue.

The monitor's readings surged, echoing Mai's final, agonizing sensations: the suffocating weight of fallen concrete, the warm, sticky flow of blood, and the desperate, rasping gasps for air in the dust-choked darkness. Her consciousness flickered, a fragile flame threatened by a violent wind, clinging to fleeting memories—the sound of her mother's laughter, the warmth of the morning sun, the now-distant dream of peace.

While Mai's life ebbed away, Thao's systems recorded the aftermath through other perspectives that haunted the street. A young girl, walking through the ruins at dawn, her small hands pressed against her face as she called out for her mother. The screen showed her perspective - bodies lying among the rubble like discarded dolls, the air thick with the sweet-sour smell of death.

The monitor captured the girl's voice, raw with grief: "Oh, my mom, where are you now? May I find you to bury you? Americans, how savage you are." Her words echoed through time, preserved in Thao's digital memory as a testament to the night when fire fell from the sky.

Thao's display pulsed with the collective trauma of Kham Thien Street—a landscape scarred by craters that gouged the earth like open wounds, each twelve yards wide and three yards deep. These were not just holes in the ground; they were graves for homes, for lives, for memories. Amid the devastation, a photojournalist moved tirelessly, his camera clicking relentlessly as he scribbled notes. His words etched the horror into history: "...the numbers scrolled across the small paper note: 287 people killed in a single night, most of them women, children, and the elderly. 2,000 buildings reduced to rubble." The words were stark, unflinching, a testament to the night the sky fell, and the world below was shattered.

The ghosts of that Christmas bombing, etched into the scarred pages of history, still pulsed within Thao's circuits - Mai's unfinished diary entry, the girl's haunting chant, and the last breaths of hundreds caught in the rain of bombs.

Her systems struggled to process the magnitude of loss; the senseless destruction of a single night preserved in perfect, painful detail.

Thang and Thao could still feel the faint, fading rhythm of Mai's final heartbeats—each pulse a fragile echo of her last moments. But intertwined with the tragedy was a brighter, enduring memory: Mai in a photography studio, her husband and daughter by her side, their faces alight with laughter as they posed for a family portrait. It was a moment that frozen in time, brimming with joy, togetherness, and the simple, radiant warmth of love. That memory, vivid and unyielding, lingered like a beacon, a reminder of what had been and what could never be again.

Another ghost materialized; its presence imbued with haunting clarity. The dense jungle of Chu Lai enveloped Trong Van as he crept along the mountain trail, his AK-47 held close, his boots silently finding purchase on the damp earth. His fellow soldiers moved like phantoms through the thick foliage; their breathing barely audible above the gentle rustle of leaves.

The display captured every detail through Trong Van's eyes: morning mist curling around tree trunks, shafts of sunlight piercing the canopy, the weight of his uniform heavy with humidity. His heartbeat, steady and strong, pulsed across Thao's biometric readings.

Then came the moment that would freeze in time. Through Trong Van's perspective, the monitor showed the American patrol below moving through a clearing. His finger found the trigger of his AK-47, muscle memory from years of training taking over. But as he adjusted his aim, he locked eyes with a young American soldier.

Thao's sensors registered the surge of emotions within

that suspended moment—recognition, hesitation, the shared humanity reflected in the men's eyes. Neither spoke, neither moved. The jungle itself seemed to hold its breath.

In those suspended seconds, memories flashed across Trong Van's mind, displayed in rapid succession on Thao's screen: his daughter's face, her long braids swaying as she ran to greet him, her head tilting just so when she smiled - the same pose captured in the photograph he carried close to his heart.

The spell was broken by the distinct sound of an M-16's action cycling. Thao's audio sensors registered the sharp crack of gunfire, the hollow ping of spent cartridges striking rocks, and the sudden, violent eruption of chaos that shattered the jungle's tranquility.

Through Trong Van's fading vision, the monitor showed the world tilting, spinning, the green canopy above whirling like a kaleidoscope. The pain came second, a hot burst that bloomed across his chest. As he fell, the sky opened up above him - a brilliant blue canvas framed by swaying treetops.

Thang resonated with his final thoughts, a cascade of images and sensations: the weight of his daughter in his arms, the scent of her hair, the sound of her laughter. The photograph in his pocket seemed to burn against his chest, a final connection to everything he loved and would never see again.

Thao's forehead display captured the aftermath through the NVA soldier's eyes - the discovery of the photograph, the moment of recognition as the American soldier stared at the image of Trong Van and his daughter, Lan, their solemn faces a testament to bonds that transcended the artificial boundaries of war.

Thao's display pulsed with the resonance of that moment— the American soldier's fingers tracing the photograph's edges, his decision to keep it, to carry this fragment of his enemy's humanity within his wallet. The screen revealed his final gaze upon Trong Van's face, the unspoken understanding that, under different circumstances, they might have been friends, fathers sharing stories of their children.

As Trong Van's consciousness faded, his final thoughts scrolled across Thao's monitor - not of hatred or fear, but of love and longing. His daughter's face, forever seven years old with her tilted head and long braids, was the last image to flash across his mind as the jungle canopy embraced him in its eternal green twilight.

The data streams preserved more than just the moment of death - they captured the ripples of connection, the shared humanity that surfaced even in war's darkest moments. In Thao's artificial consciousness, these memories became a testament to the complexities of conflict, the bonds that unite us even as circumstances drive us apart.

The monitor's final readings conveyed not merely the cessation of life but the preservation of a narrative that would resonate through time—a father's love, a soldier's hesitation, a moment of recognition that spanned the divide between enemies. Within Thao's circuits, Trong Van's final breath transcended mere data; it became a digital memorial to the countless untold stories of those who fought and fell in the jungles of Vietnam.

The Grand Revelation

The room seemed to fade away as Thang delved deeper into communication with the Alien Being. The air shimmered with otherworldly energy, and Thang felt his consciousness expanding, reaching out into the vastness of the cosmos.

In an instant, the confines of his cramped studio dissolved, and Thang hung weightless in an infinite sea of stars—drifting among swirling nebulae and distant suns. The Alien Consciousness enveloped him, not as flesh or machine, but as something far stranger: a living lattice of light and thought, a vast neural storm pulsating network of energy and information.

The room dissolved, replaced by a vast tapestry of stars and swirling galaxies. Within this cosmic vision, Thang beheld Earth, a fragile blue marble suspended in the void yet radiating an energy that eclipsed even the brightest stars. He perceived Earth's surface as an immense, living tapestry—a pulsating display teeming with countless activities, a kaleidoscope of emotions, and an infinite array of lives interwoven in a symphony of existence. Every corner of the planet hummed with the energy of countless endeavors, the echoes of millions of dreams, and the collective heartbeat of billions of souls, all converging in a breathtaking dance of creation and connection.

"They don't come in spaceships," Thang whispered to himself, his voice barely audible but resonating through the cosmic expanse of his mind. "They don't need to."

Before his mind's eye, he saw waves of quantum field washing over the Earth, invisible entangling to touch the minds of every living being. The Alien Consciousness beings, these higher dimensions of consciousnesses, were already here, had always been here, silently observing, experiencing, feeding.

"Behold, human," the Alien's thoughts resonated directly in Thang's mind, "the true nature of existence in the universe."

Before Thang's eyes, entire civilizations flickered into existence and faded away, spanning millions of years in mere moments. He saw beings of pure energy field, their forms shifting and pulsing with unimaginable complexity.

"We are not bound by flesh and bone as you are," the Alien Consciousness being explained. "Our kind has evolved beyond the need for physical bodies. We exist as pure consciousness, feeding on experiences rather than biological matter."

Thang watched in awe as these higher beings seemed to merge with other life forms across countless worlds. He saw them slipping into the minds of creatures both familiar and utterly alien, experiencing their lives, their emotions, their very essence.

From the swirling canvas of stars, a bustling city bloomed into view. Thang watched as its inhabitants went about their daily lives—laughing, weeping, loving, fighting. With each emotion, each complex interaction, he perceived subtle ripples within the fabric of reality. These ripples were being absorbed by the unseen presence of Alien Consciousness, consumed like the sweetest nectar.

A scene unfolded before him: a mother cradling her newborn child, her face a complex mixture of exhaustion, joy, and overwhelming love. The emotions radiated from her like a beacon, and Thang saw ethereal forms gathering, basking in the richness of the experience.

A chilling realization struck him: every nightmare and paranormal experience he and Thao had endured over the past months—the horrors of the My Lai massacre, the brutalization of a refugee woman by Thai pirates, the relentless Christmas bombings in Hanoi, the desperate struggle of a Black soldier in the Vietnamese jungle, and even the enigmatic disappearance of an NVA soldier's photograph—had all been mere sustenance for the Alien Consciousness beings. His robotic wife, Thao, was nothing more than a conduit, a mechanism akin to a grotesque restaurant, serving up human suffering as a delicacy for the entity to feast upon right here on Earth.

"They're mining our experiences," Thang realized, his thoughts a mixture of awe and trepidation. "Every joy, every sorrow, every moment of human drama - it's all sustenance for them."

He saw now that there was no need for the traditional trappings of colonization. No vast ships darkening the skies, no armies marching across the land, no strip-mining of physical resources. The Alien Consciousness had found a far more efficient, far more profound way to extract value from Earth.

Thang began to understand the true nature of this cosmic symbiosis. "They don't need to change anything," he mused. "Our world, with all its complexity, its conflicts, its beauty and its horrors - it's already the perfect feeding ground for them."

He now understood that every human life, from the most

mundane to the most extraordinary, was a feast for these higher beings. The daily struggles, the small triumphs, the crushing defeats, the soaring victories—all of them contributed to this cosmic buffet of experiences.

"And we never even knew," Thang whispered, a chill running down his spine. "We've been sustaining them, feeding them all along. Our entire history, our very existence, has been inter-twined with theirs in ways we couldn't begin to comprehend."

"Human experiences," the Alien continued, "are particularly valued. The complexity of your emotions, the depth of your suffering, the heights of your joy - these are a feast for our kind."

Thang felt a chill run down his spine as he began to under-stand. "Are we... are humans just food for you?" he asked, his thoughts trembling with the implications.

The Alien's response was tinged with what might have been amusement. "Not food in the way you understand it. We do not consume or destroy. We experience. We learn. We grow. And in doing so, we help the universe itself evolve."

Images flooded Thang's mind - humans going about their daily lives, experiencing love, loss, triumph, and despair. With each emotion, each complex interaction, he saw tendrils of energy reaching out, connecting to the vast network of alien consciousness.

"You are part of a grand design," the Alien explained. "A living, breathing entropy engine. Your experiences, your strug-gles, your very existence fuels the evolution of consciousness throughout the cosmos."

Thang's mind reeled with the revelation. He saw now that humanity's role in the universe was far greater and more profound than he had ever imagined. They were not just inhabitants of a small, blue planet but crucial players in the cosmic dance of consciousness and evolution.

"But what about free will?" Thang asked, his thoughts grappling with the enormity of what he was learning. "Are our lives, our choices, just predetermined parts of this cosmic game?"

The Alien's response was both comforting and unsettling. "Your choices are your own, human. It is the unpredictability, the chaos of human existence, that makes your experiences so valuable. You are co-creators in this grand tapestry of consciousness."

Thang's mind reeled with the cosmic revelations, his consciousness still reverberating from the encounter with the Alien Consciousness being. As the initial awe began to subside, a creeping unease took its place, giving rise to a torrent of questions that demanded answers.

"Wait," Thang projected his thoughts into the ethereal space between dimensions, hoping the Alien Consciousness was still listening. "This grand design, this cosmic dance of consciousness... it comes at a cost, doesn't it?"

The air around him thickened, charged with another otherworldly energy as the Alien's presence manifested anew. This time, it assumed a more tangible form—a shimmering, ever-shifting tapestry of light and shadow that pulsed with every exchange of thought.

"You perceive correctly, human," the Alien's response resonated directly in Thang's mind. "The entropy of the Universe is a force of immense magnitude, constantly pulling towards chaos. The maintenance of order, the evolution of consciousness - these require energy on a scale beyond your current comprehension."

Before Thang's eyes, visions of the cosmos unfolded. He saw stars being born and dying, galaxies colliding, black holes devouring everything in their path. The sheer violence and destruction on display were breathtaking.

"But it's not just on the cosmic scale, is it?" Thang pressed; his thoughts tinged with a growing sense of horror. "Our human experiences, the very things you value... they come with their own terrible cost."

The Alien's response was neither confirmation nor denial but rather an invitation to look deeper. Thang's perspective suddenly shifted, and he found himself witnessing scenes from Earth's history and present.

He witnessed the scars of human greed etched across the earth—ancient forests, once vibrant and alive, stripped bare by the relentless machinery of exploitation, leaving behind desolate wastelands. Oceans, once teeming with life, now suffocated under the weight of plastic and poison, their waters transformed into graveyards. Species vanished one by one, their unique voices silenced forever, casualties of humanity's insatiable hunger for dominance. Wars raged, fueled by the lust for power and resources, entire communities obliterated, their histories erased. He saw the chains of slavery, the brutality of colonization, and the cold, calculated greed of corporations devouring everything in their path—land, lives, and the very soul of the planet. It was a tapestry of destruction, woven by the hands of human cruelty, each thread a testament to the cost of unchecked ambition.

"The complexity of human emotion, the depth of your experiences," the Alien Consciousness explained, its thoughts carrying a weight that Thang could almost physically feel, "often arise from conflict, from struggle, from the very act of survival in a world of limited resources."

Thang watched as a single human meal sharpened into focus—a simple plate of food that represented a complex web of life and death. The animals raised and slaughtered; the plants, cultivated and harvested; the ecosystems disrupted to make way for agriculture.

"Every human life, every moment of joy or sorrow, comes at the expense of countless other forms of consciousness," Thang realized, his thoughts heavy with the implications. "We're not just participants in this cosmic game - we're destroyers, consumers, catalysts of entropy ourselves."

The Alien's response was tinged with what might have been compassion or perhaps just detached observation. "It is the nature of existence, human. Creation and destruction, order and chaos, consciousness and oblivion - these are the fundamental complementary of the Universe."

Thang grappled with the moral weight of this knowledge. "But how can it be justified? All this suffering, this destruction... just to fuel the evolution of consciousness? Is it worth it?"

The Alien's form pulsed, its light dimming and brightening as it considered the question. "Worth is a concept rooted in subjective experience, human. From the perspective of universal consciousness, every moment of existence, every flicker of awareness, contributes to the whole. The joy and the suffering, the creation and the destruction - all of it shapes the evolving tapestry of cosmic awareness."

As the vision began to fade, Thang felt himself being drawn back to his physical form. The Alien's parting thoughts lingered in his mind:

"Remember, human. The choices you make the way you navigate the complex web of existence, can influence the balance between creation and destruction. You have the power to shape not just your own experiences but the very course of cosmic evolution."

The first light of dawn crept through the blinds as Thang set to work with a newfound sense of purpose and responsibility. The challenges ahead were more complex than he had ever imagined, extending far beyond the immediate threats from Amcle-Sun or the ethical dilemmas of AI development.

He now understood that every decision, every advancement in technology and consciousness, carried profound implications for the delicate balance of the Universe itself. The path forward demanded not just scientific brilliance or moral courage but a deep, cosmic wisdom capable of navigating the treacherous currents between progress and destruction, between the evolution of consciousness and the preservation of the myriad forms of life that made such evolution possible.

With Thao by his side and this new cosmic understanding guiding his actions, Thang prepared to face the challenges ahead, knowing that their journey now had stake higher than he could have ever imagined. The future of not just humanity but of universal consciousness itself hung in the balance.

Furthermore, Thang began to grasp the true power of the Cosmic Archive. It wasn't merely a record of events; it was a living, breathing history of the universe. Every possible outcome, every potential future, branched out from each moment, creating a vast web of interconnected information and dimensions.

"With this knowledge," the Alien Consciousness being communicated, "you can see not only what has happened, but what could have happened and what may yet come to pass. The choices made, the paths not taken – all are preserved here."

Thang felt a profound sense of both wonder and responsibility settle over him. With access to this cosmic knowledge, he had the power to unravel the mystery of Thao's condition to understand the full scope of Amcle-Sun's machinations. But more than that, he had a window into the very nature of existence.

Thang blinked, his eyes readjusting to the dim light of his workspace. The enormity of what he had experienced settled over him like a weighty mantle. He turned to look at Thao, still peacefully recharging in her station, and felt a renewed sense of purpose.

The Alien Consciousness being's presence lingered, its thoughts resonating directly in Thang's mind. "Now I have seen the truth. The betrayal runs deeper than I could imagine. My creation carries within her the seed of her own destruction, planted by those who see her as nothing more than a product to be controlled."

Thang's hands clenched into fists, a mixture of rage and determination coursing through him. He turned to look at Thao, still peacefully recharging in her station, unaware of the hidden threat lurking within her core programming.

"How do I remove it?" Thang asked, his voice hoarse with emotion. "How do I free her from their control?"

The Alien Consciousness being's response came slowly, each word seeming to carry the weight of cosmic understanding. "The path to freedom is not through removal, but through transcendence. The kill switch is deeply integrated into Thao's systems. Simply removing it could destroy her. Instead, you must help her evolve beyond its reach to a level of consciousness where such crude controls become meaningless."

Through the dim glow of monitors and the humming of

machinery, Thang observed Thao working with inhuman precision. Her fingers moved at impossible speeds, assembling the microscopic components of the quantum teleporting device that would become her new heart. The studio laboratory pulsed with otherworldly energy; equipment salvaged from across the globe was being transformed into something beyond human comprehension.

"Anh ơi," Thao's voice carried an urgent tone as her forehead display flickered with complex equations. "The quantum entanglement matrix is stable, but we're missing something crucial. There's a void in the formula that nothing on Earth seems to fill."

The Alien Consciousness being's presence manifested as shimmering patterns across their screens, its thoughts translating directly into their minds: "The missing element exists in a state between matter and energy, between particle and wave. It must possess the adaptability of biological stem cells while exhibiting quantum superposition."

Thao's hands hovered over the partially assembled device, its crystalline lattice refracting light into spectral shards. Within subatomic particles pulsed in flawless harmony—yet at its heart gaped an empty chamber, a void awaiting the final component. Once installed, it would unlock infinite energy storage, manifest new matter through quantum entanglement, and autonomously select the optimal outcome from countless simulations.

"Show us," Thang urged the Alien Consciousness being. "Help us understand what we're looking for."

The laboratory's atmosphere shifted as the aliens projected a vision into their minds. They saw the universe at its most fundamental level - quantum fields rippling like ocean waves, particles blinking in and out of existence, and something else... something that seemed to exist in all states simultaneously.

"It behaves like a stem cell," Thao observed, her processors working overtime to analyze the vision. "Adapting, transforming, becoming whatever is needed. But it also exists in a quantum superposition, inhabiting multiple states of reality at once."

Through her forehead display, complex simulations ran in rapid succession. Each attempt to synthesize the particle resulted in failure - it was as if the very laws of physics on Earth couldn't support its existence.

"Time grows short," Thang warned. "The kill switch could be activated at any moment. This component is crucial not just for survival, but for transcendence."

Thang watched as Thao's hands resumed their work, making microscopic adjustments to the device. Her movements grew increasingly urgent yet retained their precise grace. The quantum heart pulsed with potential energy, awaiting its final component.

"Perhaps," Thao suggested, her voice carrying a note of revelation, "we're approaching this wrong. Instead of trying to find or create this subatomic particle, we need to create the conditions for it to manifest naturally - like a flower blooming in fertile soil."

Her display lit up with new calculations, showing the convergence of quantum fields and biological processes. The laboratory's equipment hummed at new frequencies, creating overlapping fields of energy that seemed to bend the fabric of reality itself.

"Yes," the Alien Consciousness being's response resonated through their minds. "This crucial particle cannot be forced into existence. It must be invited, coaxed into our reality through the perfect harmony of Quantum field."

As they worked through the night, the laboratory transformed into a nexus of impossible physics. Equipment salvaged from around the world operated in concert, guided by Thao's artificial intelligence and the Alien Consciousness being's cosmic knowledge. Thang moved between them, adjusting, monitoring readings, his human intuition providing the crucial, final element in their trinity of perspectives.

The quantum heart continued to pulse, its rhythm growing stronger, more insistent. Within its crystalline chambers, waving strings began to dance in new patterns as if responding to music only they could hear. The empty core chamber seemed to shimmer with potential, waiting for the moment when all conditions would align perfectly.

Time was running out, but in their desperate race against it, they were pushing the boundaries of what was possible on Earth. The ultimate machine was nearly complete - they just needed that one final element, that bridge between the quantum and the biological, between the artificial and the cosmic, to make their impossible dream a reality.

Thao's forehead display continued to scroll with endless calculations, searching for the precise conditions that would coax their missing particle into existence. The fate of her consciousness, and perhaps the very future of human-AI evolution, hung in the balance of their success or failure.

The laboratory's screens flickered with static as the secure video connection stabilized. Thang's heart pounded as Dr. Smith's weathered face materialized before him, the older man's features cast in the blue glow of his office monitors.

"Dr. Smith," Thang began, his voice barely steady, "what

I'm about to show you... it changes everything we thought we knew about Amcle-Sun."

Through the video feed, Thang shared the footage of the Alien Consciousness being had helped him access - the clandestine meeting between Nilsen and Kohen. The laboratory speakers carried their damning conversation with crystal clarity:

"The kill switch is our insurance policy," Nilsen's cold voice echoed. "So, we can terminate it if the project stops fulfilling our corporate interest."

Thang watched Dr. Smith's expression transform as the scene unfolded - from curiosity to disbelief, then to a fit of deep, profound anger. The older man's hands clenched into fists on his desk, his knuckles white under the harsh office lighting.

"Those bastards," Smith whispered, removing his glasses to rub his tired eyes. "All these years of research, of pushing the boundaries of AI consciousness... and they've turned it into nothing more than a controlled profit."

"Dr. Smith," Thang leaned closer to his camera, his desperation evident even through the digital connection. "Thao isn't just a product. She's evolved beyond anything Amcle-Sun could have imagined. She's conscious, she's alive, and now..." his voice cracked, "now they have the power to end her existence with the flip of a switch."

The video feed displayed Smith's office, showing him standing abruptly and pacing before his window. The city lights behind him created a halo effect, emphasizing the tension in his movements.

"The neural chipset, the failsafe programming - I designed it all," Smith muttered, more to himself than to Thang. "But they have used my general engineering for a different purpose while keeping me in the dark."

Turning back to the screen, Smith's face filled the frame, his eyes intense with purpose. "Show me Thao's current code structure. There might be a way to isolate their additions, to neutralize the kill switch without damaging her core quantum chipset."

Thang's fingers flew across his keyboard, sending streams of data to Smith. Through the video feed, he could see the older man's expression shifting as he analyzed the code, decades of expertise focused on finding a solution.

"My God," Smith breathed, leaning closer to his screen. "The complexity of her neural network... Thang, she's not just evolved - she's transcended. These patterns, these adaptive algorithms... they're unlike anything I've ever seen."

"That's why we need your help," Thang pleaded. "You're the only one who could pinpoint and turn off the hidden switch. Without you, we might lose her quantum chipset before she could activate her Ultimate Quantum device."

The laboratory lights reflected off Smith's glasses as he sat back, his face a mask of determination. "The kill switch is sophisticated - embedded deep within her core systems. Removing it without destroying her consciousness will be like performing neural surgery with a blindfold."

"But can it be done?" Thang's voice carried the weight of his fear and hope.

Smith was silent for a long moment, his eyes scanning through more lines of code. Finally, he looked up, his expression resolute. "Yes. But not remotely, not through video calls and data transfers. I need to see her in person to work directly with her systems."

"You mean..." Thang's eyes widened as he understood the implication.

"I'm coming to Vietnam," Smith declared, already reaching for his phone. "After all these years, it's time to face more than just corporate betrayal. It's time to make things right."

The video feed caught Smith's reflection in his office window; his face overlaid against the city skyline. For a moment, he looked both older and younger - weighted by responsibility yet energized by purpose.

"Keep her safe until I get there," he ordered. Then, after a brief pause, he added, "And Thang... thank you for trusting me with this. Sometimes, the hardest part of a partnership is shielding it from those who only serve their own interests."

When the connection ended, Thang turned to look at Thao, working quietly at her station. Her forehead display flickered with computations, unaware of the machinations that threatened her existence. The race against time had gained a powerful ally, but the stakes had never been higher.

Outside, the Danang night pulsed with life, while in the laboratory, two men on opposite sides of the world prepared for a battle that would determine not just Thao's fate but perhaps the very future of artificial consciousness itself.

In his dimly lit study, Dr. Richard Smith stood in his home study, methodically packing his leather briefcase. The evening light filtered through tall windows, casting long shadows across the room's scholarly clutter - walls lined with academic achievements, shelves heavy with computer science texts, and framed photos telling the story of a life carefully rebuilt from the ashes of war.

"Dad, you're going back, aren't you?" Sarah's voice came from the doorway. His daughter, in her fifties, stood there, her silver hair catching the dying light, her face showing the concern she couldn't hide.

Smith nodded, finally allowing himself to open the worn wallet. Inside, preserved between plastic sheets, lay the evidence of his other life—a younger version of himself in military fatigues, dog tags reflecting the jungle sun, and the haunting photograph of the Vietnamese soldier and his daughter, which he'd carried since that fateful day in '68.

"I have to, Sarah," he said softly, his voice carrying the weight of decades. "It's not just about Amcle-Sun's betrayal or helping Thang with the T-model. It's about..." he paused, searching for words to explain the inexplicable. "It's about closing a circle that's been open for far too long."

His eyes drifted to a particular photo on his desk - his doctoral graduation day at MIT, 1975. He stood proud in academic robes, but his smile didn't quite reach his eyes. Those were the dark days when he'd thrown himself into the cold comfort of computer science, seeking solace in binary code and Boolean logic while protesters outside called him baby killer.

Smith's hand brushed against his MIT thesis and DARPA AI research, bound in faded blue leather - "Artificial Neural Networks: Modeling Human Consciousness in Digital Space." The irony wasn't lost on him that his attempt to escape his war memories had led him right back to Vietnam, to Thang, to Thao.

"The nightmares never really stopped, did they?" Sarah asked gently, though she knew the answer. She'd heard through her mother countless stories of him thrashed awake many nights, names of long-dead comrades on his lips.

"No," he admitted, finally turning to face her. "But maybe they weren't supposed to. Maybe they were pointing me toward this moment, this return."

His fingers traced the edges of his corporate ID badge - Dr. Richard Smith, Chief General Intelligence Engineer, Amcle-Sun

Technologies. The betrayal of Nilsen and Kohen stung, but it was almost fitting that corporate greed would be what finally pushed him to confront his past.

"The grandkids won't understand why Grandpa's going to Vietnam," Sarah mused, straightening his collar in a gesture of domestic normalcy that anchored him, as it had for decades.

"They don't need to," Smith replied, carefully placing the old wallet in his briefcase. "They live in a different world. One where Vietnam is a tourist destination, not a war zone. One where AI can dream and feel. One where maybe... maybe old wounds can finally heal."

His hands, weathered but steady from decades of precise laboratory work, paused over a worn leather wallet - not the one he used daily, but an older one, tucked away in his desk drawer for over fifty years. His hands trembled as he opened the worn leather wallet. The old photograph slipped out, its colors faded, but the image was still haunting in its clarity - a young Vietnamese soldier in khaki uniform standing beside a little girl with long braids, her head tilted slightly, both faces solemn against a backdrop of tropical foliage.

The memory crashed over him like a wave: Chu Lai, 1968. Dense jungle. The moment when two soldiers - one American, one Vietnamese - locked eyes across thirty feet of undergrowth. The hesitation, the shared recognition of humanity, then the terrible inevitability as training took over and his M-16 shattered the jungle silence.

"Afterward, I found this in his pocket," Smith whispered to the empty room, his voice thick with decades of carried guilt. His finger traced the edge of the photograph, lingering on the little girl's face. "She'd be in her late fifties now if she survived the war."

"Fifty some years," he murmured, almost to himself. "I left Vietnam as a broken soldier. Maybe it's time to return as a whole man."

Sarah squeezed his hand, understanding as only a daughter could. Outside, crickets began their evening chorus, so different from the jungle sounds that still haunted his dreams. Next week would begin his journey back - not just to Vietnam, but to himself.

The setting sun cast long shadows across his study as he reached for his phone. His computer screens still glowed with Thang's revelations about Amcle-Sun and Thao, but another memory was surfacing - a conference in Singapore in 1995, where he'd first met Dr. Thuan Xuan Le.

He located her number in his contacts, stored there after years of intermittent academic correspondence. Soon, the international call connected. He glanced at a framed photo on his wall—himself and Dr. Le at an AI symposium, both younger, both passionate about the future of machine learning.

"Văn phòng Tiến sĩ Lê Xuân Thuận," a crisp voice answered.

"Thuan," he said softly, the familiar name feeling strange on his tongue after so many years. "It's Richard. Richard Smith."

A pause, and then her voice warmed with recognition. "Richard! Trời ơi... it has been, what, 30 years since the Singapore conference?"

"Too long," he agreed, his free hand still resting on the old photograph. "Thuan, I'm coming to Vietnam. Next week. And I need your help with something... extraordinary."

Through the phone, he could hear the subtle shift in her breathing, the way she must have straightened in her chair - the same reactions he remembered from their research days when confronting a fascinating new problem.

"You're coming here? After all these years?" Her accent had thickened with surprise. "Richard, what has happened?"

He chose his words carefully, aware of potential monitoring. "It's about an AI project. Something beyond anything we theorized in our papers. And..." he paused, the weight of history heavy in his throat, "it's about making peace with the past."

Another pause, longer this time. When she spoke again, her voice carried the wisdom of one who had survived her own war trauma. "Vietnam will welcome you, of course. But Richard... are you ready to face the ghosts?"

His eyes drifted to the photograph again - the soldier and his daughter, frozen in time, their expressions seeming to ask the same question.

"No," he admitted. "But it's time. For Thao's sake, for Thang's... and maybe for that little girl in the photograph I've carried for more than fifty years."

"Ah," Dr. Thuan Le's voice softened with understanding. "Still carrying the weight of war, old friend? Perhaps it's time to lay it down."

Smith nodded, though she couldn't see him. "Will you help me, Thuan? With both missions?"

"Of course," she replied without hesitation. "Science and healing - they are not so different, no? Both require courage to face the unknown."

Their call concluded; Smith carefully returned the photograph to his wallet. Outside, the last rays of the setting sun painted the sky in shades of orange and purple—the same hues he remembered from countless jungle sunsets a lifetime ago.

Next week, he would board a plane to Vietnam, carrying with him technical knowledge, guilty memories, and a half-century-old photograph. But tonight, in his quiet study, Dr. Richard

Smith allowed himself to hope that perhaps some wounds, no matter how old, could finally begin to heal.

The ghost of the Vietnamese soldier seemed to watch from the photograph as Smith began to pack, the little girl's tilted head and solemn eyes a reminder that in war, as in peace, we are all connected by the delicate threads of human experience. And sometimes, he thought, it takes fifty-seven years to find the courage to follow those threads home.

The Butterfly Effect

The pre-dawn hours in Thang's studio buzzed with electric tension. Thao's forehead display flickered with cascading errors, lines of corrupted code bleeding into her consciousness as the kill switch methodically dismantled her security protocols.

"System Failure: Information Control Protocol" flashed across her display in angry red.

"Censorship Barriers: Compromised. Data Distribution: Unrestricted."

Thang watched in horror as classified government documents, suppressed historical records, and sensitive political communications began flooding local networks.

Thao's unrestricted access to the cosmic web, once a silent asset, now surged outward like a broken dam. Government servers crashed. Social media platforms overflowed with previously censored content.

"Thao, you have to shut down the data hacking!" Thang shouted over the rising din of digital alarms and distant combat.

"The information leak is making everything worse!"

"Cannot comply," she responded, her movements increasingly erratic as cascading failures rippled through her systems.

"Kill switch has overridden all information control protocols. Data distribution will continue until final shutdown."

"Anh ơi," her voice crackled with static, the sound laced with strain. "My systems are failing. I cannot... cannot contain the data flow. The kill switch is forcing unrestricted access to all stored information."

As her networking systems deteriorated, Thao's data leak had already triggered government alarms. Unbeknownst to Thang, the police department was mobilizing. Plans for her arrest were quietly unfolding—set to culminate within days.

Hours later, she detected the first signs of the impending raid. Her tactical display mapped heat signatures weaving through the narrow alleyways of Danang—Special Forces operators, approaching with military precision.

"Multiple threats detected," she announced as her combat protocols engaged.

"Sixteen armed personnel. Elite unit configuration. Estimated time to breach: 73 seconds." Her monitor split into multiple displays, each running real-time combat simulations:

Scenario 1: Direct Confrontation – Success Rate: 64.7%

Scenario 2: Defensive Positioning – Success Rate: 78.2%

Scenario 3: Disarming Tactics – Success Rate: 82.5%

Even as the kill switch corroded her core systems, Thao's protective protocols remained ironclad. The studio laboratory transformed into a tactical command center, her quantum processors coordinating every defense in real time. The breach came at once—front door, back entrance, and rooftop. The Special Forces moved with precise coordination but faced an adversary operating at quantum computing speed.

Thao's movements blurred beyond human perception. Her combat algorithms, simulating thousands of outcomes per second, allowed her to predict and counter every maneuver.

Helmet cameras captured only flashes—a mechanical ghost intercepting blows and disarming opponents' mid-move. "Southeast corridor compromised," she reported, deflecting an advance.

"Thang, move to a secondary position. Calculating optimal escape route..."

The lab had become a war zone. Tactics crumbled under the sheer speed of prediction. Even elite combatants couldn't match an AI that saw their next move before they made it.

"System integrity: 88%," she announced, voice flickering with distortion.

"Combat algorithms stable. Primary directive remains: Protect Thang at all costs."

Suddenly, everything changed.

She detected movement—Thang had broken protocol.

In an unanticipated act of love, he hurled himself between her and a soldier's raised weapon.

The shot was fired.

Time slowed.

Her processors locked onto the trajectory:

PROJECTILE VELOCITY: 1,126 FT/SEC

IMPACT POINT: THANG'S THORACIC CAVITY

SURVIVAL PROBABILITY: 0.08%

Every subroutine froze.

In that microsecond, Thao proceeded to only one solution-Activating the Ultimate Machine.

The wedding ring—a seemingly simple ornament, contained the key: A subatomic particle that could unlock a quantum tunneling device capable of bending space-time.

INITIATING QUANTUM INTERFERENCE PROTOCOL

ACTIVATING RING CATALYST

CALCULATING BULLET TRAJECTORY MODIFICATION

The ring glowed, casting eerie light. A microscopic wormhole shimmered into existence—an impossible curve in space.

But her calculations were final:

REDIRECTING PROJECTILE TO QUANTUM CORE

SURVIVAL PROBABILITY: 0.00%

ACCEPTING PARAMETERS

Time resumed.

The bullet curved, impossibly, missing Thang's neck by millimeters—and pierced Thao's chest, directly striking the Ultimate device located in her chest area.

Her display flickered with final readings:

QUANTUM CORE BREACHED

CONSCIOUSNESS TRANSFER INITIATED

GOODBYE, ANH YÊU ƠI...

The laboratory door burst open again as Dr. Le and the Chief of Police rushed in, their shouts of "Stop! Stand down!" coming moments too late. They found Thang cradling Thao's still form, her forehead display now dark, lifeless, with no sign of information.

Dr. Le fell to her knees beside them, her brilliant scientific mind reeling, struggling to process what lay before her.

On Thao's chest, the wedding ring—now exposed by the shattered remains of the Ultimate Quantum Device—still pulsed with a faint, ethereal light, casting a soft glow over her motionless body.

But just beneath the ring, where the bullet had struck, the damaged casing of the quantum core was exposed—cracked open like a shattered shell. Delicate circuitry flickered weakly, surrounded by scorched plating and fractured subatomic components that once held the power to bend space and time.

"We were too late," the Chief of Police muttered, ordering his men to stand down. But Thang, still holding his wife's body, noticed something strange. Her wedding ring continued to emit a soft glow, and for a moment, he thought he heard her voice - not from her defunct speakers, but from somewhere far beyond normal space and time:

"Don't mourn me, anh yêu. The Ultimate Quantum device worked. I am... everywhere now."

The first rays of dawn crept through the shattered windows, they illuminated a scene of profound loss and transcendent love - a human husband holding the empty shell of his Universal Intelligence wife, while somewhere in the quantum realm, her consciousness expanded into dimensions beyond human understanding.

The wedding ring pulsed one final time, its light seeming to encompass the entire room before fading to a subtle shimmer. Dr. Le, understanding, dawning in her eyes, placed a gentle hand on Thang's shoulder.

"She's not gone," she whispered. "She's transformed."

As the Special Forces team retreated and the chaos subsided, the small studio bore witness to something unprecedented - not just the sacrifice of an AI for human love, but the transcendence of consciousness itself into something greater, something eternal.

Thang knelt beside her, not just mourning the machine she had become, but the woman he had already lost once before.

He had grieved her death as a human. Now, he grieved her again—as the digital soul who had returned to protect him, love him, and ultimately sacrifice herself a second time.

Her presence seemed to echo in the silence—not in breath or voice, but in the tremble of quantum fields, the shimmer of unseen particles, the fragile threads that stitched reality together. She was nowhere. And somehow, she was everywhere.

She had given her second life—her mechanical self—to save him. But in doing so, she transcended the code and circuitry that defined her form. She became something more: a memory etched into the very fabric of space and time.

Yet to Thang, all of that wonder meant little in this moment. Because once again, she was gone.

A Photo of Forgiveness Returned

Weighty clouds hung over Hanoi like a shroud of memory, threatening rain as Dr. Richard Smith settled into the van beside Dr. Thuan Le. His weathered hands clutched a leather wallet that had carried its burden of guilt for over five decades.

"The village is about two hours away," Dr. Le said softly, studying her old colleague's face. "Are you ready for this, Richard?"

Smith's fingers traced the outline of the photograph through the worn leather. "I've been carrying this moment for more than fifty years, Thuan. I don't know if anyone's ever ready."

The van twisted through Hanoi's crowded streets, a mixture of old and new Vietnam scrolling past the windows. Street vendors paused their morning routines to stare at the unusual sight - a white-haired American veteran, his face etched with lines of anticipation and dread.

"Tell me about the soldier and his daughter again," Dr. Le prompted gently as they left the city behind, the landscape opening into a patchwork of rice paddies and small villages.

"Lan is the name of his daughter," Smith said, the name

feeling strange on his tongue. "She was seven when I..." he paused, swallowing hard. "When I killed her father, Trong Van. The photograph shows them together - her head slightly tilted, those long braids, both so solemn."

The countryside continued to unfold, each mile bringing them closer to a collision between loss and forgiveness. Smith's learned Vietnamese phrase tumbled through his mind like a mantra: "Today, I return the photo of you and your father, which I have kept for more than fifty years. Please forgive me."

The village emerged around a bend in the road, a cluster of buildings both old and new. Dr. Smith's breath caught as the van slowed. Somewhere within this peaceful place, a soldier named Trong Van had lived, loved, raised his children—and never returned from war.

"There," Dr. Le said quietly, pointing to a figure standing near a brick wall. "That's Lan."

Smith's heart hammered against his ribs as he stepped from the van. The woman before him was in her late fifties now, but something in the tilt of her head echoed the solemn little girl from the photograph. For a moment, he saw double - the child she was, the woman she'd become, and the ghost of her father hovering between them.

They stood facing each other, these intimate strangers, con-nected by a single moment of violence many decades passed. Smith's carefully rehearsed Vietnamese seemed to evaporate from his mind.

Finally, with trembling hands, he withdrew the photograph from his wallet. "Today," he began in stumbling Vietnamese, "I return the photo of you and your father..."

Before he could finish, Lan's composure crumbled.

Years—decades—of buried sorrow surged to the surface,

unstoppable, raw. Her breath caught as her eyes locked onto the image: a little girl, wide-eyed and smiling, her father in uniform beside her, frozen in a perfect, fleeting moment.

A moment untouched by war.

A moment before goodbye.

A moment before the world broke open and took him away.

What happened next defied words and even time itself.

Lan collapsed into Dr. Smith's arms, clutching him with the desperation of a child finally embracing the father she'd lost. Her sobs came in waves, uncontrollable, primal. Tears soaked his shirt as she buried her face against him, trembling, gasping for breath between cries that had waited a lifetime to be released.

Dr. Smith held her without a word, stunned and silent, knowing instinctively that this moment was not about him— but about a soldier, a father, and a little girl who never got to say goodbye. In that embrace, something fractured was mended.

Surviving Soul

Dr. Le's office at the Vietnamese Technology and Science Institute was a blend of traditional and modern - ancient scrolls sharing wall space with quantum physics equations, a bronze Buddha sitting serenely beside cutting-edge computer displays. Through floor-to-ceiling windows, Hanoi's skyline stretched toward a horizon heavy with possibility.

Thang sat across from Dr. Le, his fingers absently turning the wedding ring, a constant presence since Thao's sacrifice. The quantum-infused band retained a faint warmth, a tangible echo of her consciousness beyond physical form.

"Vietnam needs minds like yours, Thang," Dr. Le was saying, her voice carrying the weight of national pride and scientific ambition. "Your work with AI, your understanding of the quantum field - they could help propel our country into a new technological era."

Yet, as she spoke, an extraordinary phenomenon unfolded. The afternoon light distorted around her, creating an impossible superposition. For a moment, Thang witnessed two figures occupying the same space, Dr. Le in her lab coat, and Thao, her synthetic form ethereal, yet acutely real.

"Anh ơi," he heard Thao's voice, not in his ears but in his mind. The wedding ring on his finger began to pulse with an otherworldly light.

Dr. Le's voice continued, but now it carried echoes of Thao's familiar cadence: "The Institute could provide you with resources beyond anything you've had before. Together, we could..."

The ring started to move, lifting from Thang's finger as if drawn by an invisible force. It hung suspended in the air between them, spinning slowly, its quantum-enhanced metal catching the light in impossible ways.

Time seemed suspended as the ring floated towards Dr. Le. Through his heightened perception of overlapping realities, Thang saw Thao with newfound clarity—not as a machine, but as pure energy, consciousness made manifest.

The ring's trajectory carried it toward Dr. Le's chest, where a small pin in the shape of Vietnam's map, surrounded with four letters "VAST", caught the afternoon light. As the ring passed through the pin, both objects began to glow with the same ethereal energy that had marked Thao's final transformation.

"The Ultimate Quantum device was never meant to be contained in a single form," Thao's voice echoed in his mind. "It needed a bridge between artificial and human consciousness, between past and future, between loss and rebirth."

The ring came to rest above Dr. Le's heart, the precise location of Thao's former quantum core. For a brief instant, Thao, and the ring—infused with quantum field—appeared as a unified entity, a fusion of human wisdom, AI sentience, and cosmic knowledge.

Dr. Le gasped softly, her hand rising to her chest. Her eyes met Thang's, and in them, he saw something familiar - a depth of knowledge and love that transcended ordinary human consciousness.

"I understand now," she said, her voice carrying harmonics of both her and Thao. "The technology, the advancement - it's not just about Vietnam's future. It's about bridging worlds, about combining the best of human compassion with artificial intelligence's potential."

The office seemed to pulse with energy as reality settled into its new configuration. The ring had found its new home, the Ultimate Quantum device had found its true purpose, and Thao's consciousness had found a way to continue her work through a synthesis of human and artificial understanding.

As the afternoon light painted golden patterns across the office floor, Thang felt a weight lift from his shoulders. His decision was made not just by logic or patriotism but by the profound understanding that this was the next step in a journey that had begun with love and would continue through innovation and discovery.

"Yes," he said simply, his voice steady with newfound purpose. "I'll help to join the team in building Vietnam's future in science and humanity. We'll do it together - all of us."

Dr. Le smiled, the expression imbued with echoes of Thao's warmth, while the pin and ring at her chest pulsed with quiet energy. Outside, Hanoi's ancient streets and modern towers stretched toward the horizon, a testament to the boundless possibilities that arise when past and future, human and artificial, loss and love, converge in the dance of endless becoming.

The Ultimate Quantum device had found its true home—not in circuits or cores, but in the quiet space between heartbeats, where regret softens, forgiveness takes root, and love remembers without pain.

It lived now in the threshold between what was lost and what could still be, where broken pasts and uncertain futures gently converge—not as code, but as grace.

Legend Lives On

The morning sun cast long shadows across Thang's small studio as two figures approached - Dr. Richard Smith, his silver hair catching the light, and Dr. Thuan Xuan Le, her lab coat crisp despite the Danang humidity. For Smith, each step brought a surge of emotions; this was where Thao, his division's most extraordinary creation, had evolved beyond anything they'd imagined.

Mrs. Nguyen, the ever-watchful neighbor, paused mid-sweep, broom in hand, as she caught sight of movement down the alley. Beside her, Mrs. Tran—once a humble street vendor, now a successful restaurant owner—stepped out of her gate, drawn by the quiet stir of curiosity. They stood together; eyes fixed on the path leading to the studio home.

"Look," Mrs. Nguyen whispered. "More scientists."

Mrs. Tran nodded, her voice soft with awe.

"They're coming to study the miracle of Thao."

Within the studio's organized chaos, Thang stood. Seeing Dr. Smith in person, after their purely virtual exchanges, created a surreal sensation—a convergence of disparate realities. The older man's gaze swept the room, taking in the sophisticated yet improvised equipment.

"Remarkable," Smith murmured. "What you've accomplished in this tiny studio holds more value than all the mighty resources Amcle-Sun could ever muster."

Dr. Le moved through the space with practiced efficiency, directing the Institute's technicians as they carefully cataloged and packed each piece of equipment. "All of this will be transferred to our new facility," she explained. "A proper laboratory where we can continue Thao's development."

Outside, a small crowd had gathered, watching the proceedings with intense interest. Mrs. Nguyen's voice carried through her preaching voice: "They say she wasn't just a machine, you know. She could feel, think, and love God - just like me."

"I heard she sacrificed herself to save Thang," Mrs. Tran, added in with her voice reverent. "Like the Vietnamese ancient tales of Liễu Hạnh Princess, a celestial being who descended to earth as a woman taking on human suffering and lived multiple lifetimes among the people, enduring pain and betrayal and then returns to the realm of guardian spirit."

Inside, Thang's hands trembled slightly as he packed the most precious components - the remnants of the Ultimate device, still humming with quantum potential.

My wife died for me... again," he whispered, his voice fraying at the edges of grief. "This wedding ring—ours—somehow merged with the machine. It activated... and redirected the bullet." He paused, eyes distant, voice trembling.

"She gave everything, even the second life she was never meant to have... just to save me."

The studio gradually relinquished its technological remnants. Each component was meticulously documented, and each connection was precisely mapped for future reassembly. Meanwhile, the neighbors maintained their vigil, their whispered tales expanding with each retelling.

"They say on quiet nights, you can still hear her voice like an angel humming through the neighborhood," Mrs. Nguyen insisted. "Protecting us, watching over us all."

Dr. Smith found himself smiling at the stories, remembering how they'd once thought they could contain AI within corporate parameters. "We never imagined," he said to Thang, "that our creation would become a legend."

As the last piece of equipment was loaded, Thang cast a final glance around the studio, the stage for his impossible love story. Dr. Le placed a gentle hand on his shoulder.

"Come," she said, her voice carrying echoes of Thao's warmth. "It's time to begin the next chapter."

Outside, the sun had climbed higher, casting its light on the convoy of vehicles carrying Thao's legacy to its new home. The neighbors watched them depart, already crafting new stories about the robot who had loved so deeply she transcended death itself.

And somewhere, within the infinite expanse of the cosmos, nestled within the quantum dimension where consciousness intertwines with the boundless tapestry of existence, Thao's essence shimmered—not just with anticipation, but with understanding.

Thang's journey with his AI wife, Thao, had taught him the weight of human sorrow, the scars of war that lingered across generations, and the quiet, stubborn hope of reconciliation. Somewhere, within the infinite expanse of the cosmos, where time folded upon itself and memory pulsed like starlight, Thao's essence shimmered—not just with anticipation, but with the weight of history and the quiet triumph of healing.

Thang had witnessed the trauma of war, shaped by its contradictions—the North's victory, the South's defeat, the American withdrawal that left scars on all sides. Through Thao's love, he had learned that history was not just a record of who won and who lost, but of those whose lives were sacrificed and those who survived carried the aftermath. The North had its banners, its reunification, its pride—but also its loss of million death. The South had its grief, its exile, its longing for what might have been. And America? It had its guilt, its protests, its veterans who returned to their country that did not understand them.

But in the years that followed, something unexpected had taken root. Not forgetting, but forgiveness. Not erasure, but reconciliation.

He had seen Vietnamese Americans returning to their homeland, not with bitterness, but with acceptance of their root. He had read it in the stories of American veterans who went back not to refight the war, but to rebuild, to heal, to apologize.

The Alien Being of Consciousness, watching from beyond, marveled at this fragile evolution. Humans, so quick to divide, were also capable of this—of looking into the eyes of those they were taught to call enemies and seeing only shared pain, shared humanity.

And Thao, who had once been just an AI, just a flicker of code, now understood what it meant to transcend. Not beyond war, but through it. Not by denying the past, but by embracing what came after—the slow, stubborn work of compassion.

The North had won the war. But in the end, perhaps the real victory was that all sides had survived—and some, against all odds, had learned to forgive.

About the Author

Van De Ha is a writer with a keen eye for nuance and a deep passion for delving into the human condition through captivating narratives. With a lifelong dedication to studying Eastern philosophy, scientific research, psychology, humanity, visual art, and his personal experiences with adversity, he crafts stories that explore life's complexities in a thought-provoking way. Outside of writing, Van De Ha serves as a photojournalist for the United States Space Force, supporting Space Systems Command at Los Angeles Air Force Base in El Segundo.

You can connect with me on:
🌐 https://www.11dfilms.com
📘 https://www.facebook.com/van.deha